4/-

D.J. Coppula

INTERSTELLAR TWO-FIVE

INTERSTELLAR
TWO-FIVE

JOHN RANKINE

SCIENCE FICTION BOOK CLUB
by arrangement with
DENNIS DOBSON
London 1967

This Science Fiction Book Club edition was produced
in 1967 for sale to its members only by the proprietors,
Readers Union Ltd, Aldine House, 10-13 Bedford Street,
London W.C.2 and at Letchworth Garden City, Herts.
Full details of membership may be obtained from our
London address. The book is set in 11 pt Juliana and
has been reprinted by Clarke, Doble and Brendon Ltd,
Plymouth. It was first published by Dobson Books Ltd.

INTERSTELLAR TWO-FIVE

A*

CHAPTER ONE

'WELL, that's it.'—Peter Anders lifted his head from the litter of calculations on the chart table and looked round the circle of faces—'We're here to stay then.'

There was no immediate answer as each one digested the unwelcome facts that had come out as the end product of two days careful processing of data. Anders waited with his hands relaxed on the table in front of him. After many years in the Space Service and many successful missions, it had come to him at last. It was almost a relief. Greying hair, deeply lined face set square and uncompromising in the habit of command; he would endure to the limit, and had done so in the past, where there was reasonable hope. But this was beyond argument. They did not have enough power to lift *Interstellar Two-Five* off the planet. This was the end of the line.

He could feel sorry for the other members of the executive conference. Four men and Karen Evander. He looked first at her; which was, visually, the most rewarding thing to do. She was taking it very well. Medium height, with a rather full oval face. Auburn hair, held back in a broad headband to show a high clear forehead. Good figure, shown off to advantage in a close fitting lemon yellow shirt. Slim fingers and delicate wrists. Blue-grey eyes looking steadily ahead.

On his right, the co-pilot and second in Command, Dag Fletcher. Unlucky for him to get on a trip like this first time out after his return to the company. Six years regulation stint with the Inter Galactic Security Organisation and then to end up on a simple freight run. In home waters you might say. A tall lanky young man. Rather too casual; but very able, obviously being groomed for higher command. Just now the lean, hard face was non-committal and grey eyes were hooded as Fletcher looked intently at the summary sheet.

Chad Fergusson said, 'Let's get this right, Captain. On my report of the power reserve, you calculate that we could not mount an escape velocity from Pelorus. The best we can do is to go into an orbit in this gravisphere with a faint chance of a moon landing? I can tell you now that there will only be one take off from this beat-up power pack. It's one shot or nothing and from what you say, it's nothing.' The senior engineer pushed back from the table as if he had finished with the whole business. Round faced, looking much younger than his thirty-five years and having a constant struggle to keep within the generous weight limit for space crew, he was a man who could settle happily anywhere. Probably he would be the least bothered of the whole crew by an indefinite stay on Pelorus.

'Ground you, and we'll lift off all right, Chad.' Len Robert-shaw, Senior Communications, spoke in his morose monotone. Thin faced and taut nerved, he was a living extension of his computers.

The only remaining member of the conference was John Alvirez, the chief navigator. South American born, tall, dark, volatile. He skimmed a card which he had covered with neat tiny figures into the centre of the table. 'I can only agree with Captain Anders. There is no possibility to do more. Here we stay. At least we are in pleasant company.' He looked at Karen.

From where she was sitting, Karen was able to see out of a cleared inspection port. It was almost mid-day, 1400 hours in the twenty-eight hour cycle of day and night on Pelorus. Trace gases not present in the Earth atmosphere, but not known to be injurious to Earthmen, gave the sky a pale tinge of cinnamon. In the three days since they had made their forced landing in this temperate forest land, a wide circular clearing had been made. Charred and burnt down to bare, black, powdery soil near the ship, where the retro rockets had blasted out a path for themselves. Man-made, by felling the tall spongy trees for another fifty yards.

So far, they had seen no evidence of life, but life existed on this planet and any intruder, man or animal, would have to come out in the open to reach the ship. At the edge of the clearing Miranda Dolon was walking hand in hand with Alec Ross, her latest friend. If they stayed here, she would have ample opportunity to work at her favourite hobby. The two figures diminished to puppet size from the command module window, disappeared from view. It was a pity Alvirez couldn't turn his attention to Miranda. Thinking this, Karen ignored the remark and said, 'I can only leave the calculations to the mathematicians. I have a report ready on Pelorus if you want it now.' The cool matter-of-fact voice was a snub to Alvirez; but he never gave up.

'Your voice is music in our ears, Karen. For my part, you can report all day. All night, even.'

Fletcher spoke: 'It will certainly do no harm to have any details you can give us, Karen. Go ahead.'

'There isn't a great deal in the manuals. Pelorus has never been on the list for colonisation; chiefly because of the freak magnetic fields which were responsible for our navigational errors.'

Alvirez took this as an oblique knock at his section. He stood up and gave her a deep bow. 'How charmingly you put it.' He was going on, but Fletcher interposed with, 'No one blames you, John. All the navigators contributed to the error. It was just one of those things. Go on, Karen.'

'About one sixth bigger in mass than Earth. Higher gravity; but not seriously higher from the point of view of living on it. Atmosphere acceptable and slightly oxygen rich. We are in latitude 56° North and can expect temperate climate. Low rainfall, mild winter and summer temperatures rising to about 28° Centigrade. Not unlike the Channel Islands. Temperature increases all the way to the equator as you would expect. On the equator itself, extra vehicular activity would be limited. Probably reaches 60° Centigrade. Main geographical features are three continental masses. One stretches in a band almost completely round the equator. There is a northern mass, where we are, which comes down from the polar region roughly to latitude 45° North. Then there is a similar land mass coming up from the southern pole to about 37° South. The rest of the planet is covered by salt water of a similar density to the North Atlantic. The ocean in this hemisphere is named the Polyphontine Sea. There are small island groups, but detailed charts have not been drawn. Principally because aerial photography has been restricted by low-lying mist.'

'How far are we from the equator in miles?' Anders put the question.

'As the crow flies, just over four thousand miles.' Karen flipped over the pages in her report and pulled out a folder sketch map. 'I've put us in the picture, geographically, like this.' She pushed it forward into the centre of the table.

In the short time available, it was a beautifully detailed piece of work. Almost of the standard of a printed reproduction, with coloured hatchings to bring out relief and finely printed place name. The professional cartographer's touch was evident.

'You haven't wasted any time. This will be most helpful. Thank you.' Anders studied the main features.

'We seem to be about eight hundred miles from the coast. Forest and plain. Then two thousand miles of sea and a narrow coastal strip. Then a range of mountains followed by a plateau. The equator runs roughly down the centre of the plateau at about ten thousand feet. Something like a thousand miles

from the coast.' He turned the map to read a name—
'Leucophanes—that's the name of the mountain range. Anything special about them, Karen?'

'The note in the Pilotage Manual says they have to be
seen to be believed. An unusual white rock formation.'

'Well, there it is. Has anyone any questions for Karen?'

'Geographical questions?' asked Alvirez.

Anders was unexpectedly irritable.

'Do everyone a favour, John, will you and give your mind
to this job. Unless there is anything else to bring up, I'm
going to close this meeting. We have the facts clear. Think
about it. Tomorrow at this time, we'll have a full crew
assembly to work out an acceptable plan. Talk to your people
and give them the facts. All right?'

There was a murmur of agreement round the table. Chad
Fergusson heaved himself out of the narrow seat. 'When do
we get to eat local food? There must be something to turn
into a fresh steak.'

Len Robertshaw never lost an opportunity to state the
obvious. He followed Chad out saying seriously, 'I shouldn't
go far afield yet. You never know what might be about. We'll
need to go carefully here.'

Anders moved out with, 'I'll be in my cabin, Dag, if anything comes up.'

Alvirez picked up the map and looked at it with obvious
admiration. 'Here's a beautiful island, Karen. Must be a
tropical paradise on that latitude. Labelled Tragasus Island.
Who names these things?'

'Many people. It must be nearly a hundred years since the
first ship touched down here. There haven't been many as a
matter of fact; because of the peculiar magnetic fields. But
the manuals have built up a rough picture out of the dupli-
cate logs as you know. Names are either suggested in the log
entries or dreamed up by the Pilotage Manual Staff. At one
time there was a run on classical descriptive names rather

on the lines of botanical nomenclature. If Tragasus is one of those, it should suit you.'

Alvirez appealed to Fletcher: 'What does she mean by that, Dag?'

'I think I'd call it a draw there, John. Look, I'd like a word with Karen, if you don't mind.'

'Of course I mind. But I will absent myself from felicity awhile.'

Karen said, 'So. Felicity too. Have you no heart?'

Alvirez went out saying, 'So fair and yet so cruel.'

Dag Fletcher moved over and took the chair next to the girl. 'Karen. How much detail can you dig out of those Manuals?'

'Such as?'

'The terrain between here and the coast with enough close description to sort out a practicable route. A chart detailed enough to navigate by across the Polyphontine Sea. And probably most important, how to get on to the equatorial plateau.'

Karen turned her head to look him squarely in the eyes. The reputation of the Co-Pilot had preceded him on the ship. It was known that he had been one of the most resourceful corvette commanders in the I.G.O. service and had an almost legendary reputation. There had indeed been some reservations when he was introduced to the executive committee; but they found he had no inflated opinion about himself and was a relaxed and efficient colleague. Without making any definite effort, he had established himself as a natural leader. Anders was glad to shed on to him most of the chores of command. It was a tribute that he could do it, and keep a loyal subordinate.

'There isn't that kind of information to be had. Only general descriptions. A journey like that would give invaluable data. But then it could never be got back to the Galactic Information Office.'

'Don't be too sure about that.'

Karen said uncertainly, 'Nobody has made a fuss about it, Dag, but none of us want to stay here. Don't raise false hopes.'

'Look, Karen, I don't want this talked about yet. I have the glimmer of an idea; but it will not be an easy one to sell or an easy one to carry out. I'll work on it with Len and his computers and report tomorrow. Not a word to anyone else.'

'Just as you say.'

Karen gathered in her notes and stood up. Below the yellow shirt—very brief shorts and brown legs. Just within the line dividing the slim from the sturdy, she was a ready-made model for an Ingres. Fletcher looked at her thoughtfully. It was not by accident that he had first spoken to Karen about the possibility of finding a way out of the trap. She would be the ideal adjutant for the scheme he had in mind. Absolutely efficient and, like himself, with a flair for improvising with unlikely materials, she would be able to work with data that could not be processed for the computers. And as far as he could see from her attitude to South America's great gift to woman, she was not likely to be side-tracked by the pleasure principle. He untangled his long legs and swung himself out of the chair.

'Let's catch Len before he gets involved in a steak hunt. Chad's been trying to get him on a food shooting mission ever since we came down.'

They went in single file down the narrow communication corridor which sloped steeply across the ship in a diagonal line down to the lowest entry port. After the years with I.G.O. it still surprised Dag to find women personnel on the civilian ships. Following Karen's very feminine figure, he reflected that it was a change for the better. A civilising influence. The merest suggestion of a disturbing perfume drifted back to him. There was no doubt about it, every ship should have a spatiographer.

At the entry port, he was vertically above her, on a steep

companion. He noticed, not for the first time since the landing, that unaccountable changes of light seemed to create shafts and columns in certain areas.

She said, as though she had just decided to answer, 'It's called "Y".'

'What's that?'

'My perfume. You asked what it was called and that's it. "Y".'

'Oh.' Then without fully understanding it, he realised that if she had imagined he had raised the subject, a simple 'Oh' was no reply. So he continued, 'It suits you.' He put on an official report voice. 'It adds a further attractive dimension to your persona.'

'We spatiographers aim to please.'

Outside, the mid-day temperature was pleasantly warm. Some crew men were lying sunning themselves on the felled tree trunks. Miranda and Alec Ross appeared from the edge of the forest. Her honey blonde hair was swept back in a short pony tail. She was simply dressed in a short quilted tabard of fine stiff turquoise linen with a broad belt of bronze chain link. Open at the sides, it made no secrets of a superb figure. She was looking quite delighted.

Len Robertshaw and Chad Fergusson were sitting on a log talking to the only other woman member of the crew. Susan Yardley was the eldest of the three; slim, athelete's build, with jet black straight hair which she wore short in a simple page-boy style, emphasizing classically regular features. She shared Chad's passion for Cordon Bleu cookery. They were speculating about the local fauna and as Karen and Fletcher came up she was saying, 'It's a deal, Chad. First catch your cony and I'll guarantee the hearth and skillet. I've got a pip of a recipe in my head for an old time dish that'll send you singing about the house. It just needs a lot of time and that we shall have.'

'That's the girl, Susan,' said Dag. 'Back to the cave in

one swift step. Len, can you spare a minute to work a thing out for me?'

Squeezed on the narrow operating platform of the computer bank, with Robertshaw at the control console and Karen giving the figures, Dag framed the crucial question.

'What would be the effect of a lift-off from the equatorial plateau with the power Chad says is available? Reduce total weight by the following.' Dag read from a list he had made of items which in his opinion could be jettisoned. Karen checked weights from the manifest and Len Robertshaw played the whole thing on his keyboard in an impassive silence.

Dag explained: 'There is an optimum place and time for lift-off from any planet; but Pelorus has more snags than most and we could make a ten per cent gain by choosing dead right. Now Chad gave us a fail from here in the order of about five per cent. We could convert that to a five per cent surplus. Cut the ship down to a basic shell and we've got something in hand to manœuvre with.'

Robertshaw was checking a teletape. He fed more data into his keyboard and came back with a new strip.

'Taking a point on the equatorial belt at 10,000 feet and cutting down by the weights as given, there is a satisfactory escape velocity with roughly eight per cent margin.'

'You can't make it any more?'

'I've taken the lower limit on every probable error; I can guarantee it won't be less.'

One comforting thing about having a pessimist at the computers, reflected Dag, was that you got figures that would stand any knocking. But he had been used to blasting off, even in civilian ships, with a reserve of power in the hundreds of per cent above initial thrust. It would be a very dicey thing.

'Karen, would you dig out a possible route, with what detail you have, in the most direct line from here to the plateau? I know you can't make it very elaborate. Just do what you can.'

'Check. I'll give you a copy in the morning before the full meeting.'

'Thanks a lot. And thank you, Len, for your analysis.'

'That's all right. I can't see that it gets us any nearer; but I'm not curious. I'll wait until tomorrow to hear all. Right now I'm interested in what that Yardley girl has done with the food.'

Susan Yardley coupled general supervision of the commissariat with her official position on the ship as Junior Navigation Executive. She had old fashioned views about food and would have tethered a bullock in the control module if she could have got away with it. Her ambition was to set up a barbecue within thirty minutes of a landfall and she was only held up at the moment by a complete absence of anything to cook on it.

Even when sprayed with a fixing foam to turn the carbon dust into a clean black carpet, it was not pleasant in the immediate area of the ship. Smith and Randle, the two junior crew men in the Power Section, reported to Anders that the belt of woodland thinned out within half a mile. There was a good site overlooking rolling steppe land to the horizon. They wanted the O.K. to a building project; so that they could knock together a base camp. Anders put a temporary veto on it. 'It looks as though it will come to that; but I want everyone in the ship for the next week. We haven't seen any sign of life yet; but we can be seen for miles around and sooner or later someone or something is going to come and have a look. We'll take it slowly.'

The cinnamon sky darkened to violet in the long twilight. With the falling light level, there was a heightening of the oppressive atmosphere of the wood. In spite of surface similarities, there was something about it which was different from any northern forest in these latitudes on Earth. Every member of the crew had sensed it; some more strongly than others. The silence was one element. Since their arrival, there had been no sound. But no one would have said positively that they were not being watched.

Pelorus had three small, fast moving moons no bigger than asteroids. They were conveniently spaced to give almost continuous light through the long hours of darkness. It was a feeble and eerie glow like a stare from a pale red eye; but the clearing was visible to its edge of shadow. Military habit died hard with Fletcher and he had arranged a continuous watch in the control cabin. Brilliant searchlight beams were trained to flood the clearing at the pull of a switch. To conserve power, external light was cut to a single glowing panel in the loading port and the scanner which would give a panoramic view to the horizon in every direction was cut back to a small central square which showed only the clearing.

There was little noise from the ship. The unusually heavy Van Allen layer round Pelorus had an unexpected effect on radio signals. There was almost complete refraction and both incoming and outgoing waves went into a zigzagging circular orbit; so that no programmes could be received even from Talos, the other planet in this solar system. Talos had been their destination. It was smaller than Pelorus. Smaller even than Earth but the home of a very advanced culture.

Craig, Chad Fergusson's principal assistant, was on duty. He fed a microtape into the report reader and listened to a new novel. It had been a best-seller when they left Europe six months ago and the Space Corporation prided itself on having the most up to date libraries on its ships of any deep space line. Somebody had picked a honey of a voice to read it. Cool and dispassionate, with a hint of husky depths. Craig put his feet up and began a methodical job of filling an old briar pipe. It was an historical novel; set way back. Somebody was getting very steamed up about the foreign policy of a country with an improbable sounding name and a woman was being intelligent and helpful and understanding about it. Later, Marcia was wondering desperately what Nigel had told Alex to make him so beastly to Penny. It was sickening. Even with the voice. If life was ever as dim as that, it was a good thing time passed. His pipe began to draw smoothly. He flicked off the reader and pulled up the transparent storage tube. There was nothing else that looked even remotely interesting amongst the new titles and he let the tube fall back with a gentle pneumatic plop.

Somewhere down below in one of the two small wardrooms, a squeeze box started up with a nostalgic tune. Probably Dan Munro. He was second man in the Communications section and used the computers to write basic music. This one sounded as though he had fed in every sentimental gimmick in every popular tune in the galaxy and come up with the essence of them all. It would tear the heart out of a zombie. Craig stood up irritably and edged round the control room to an outside port. It added nothing to the view on the scanner. In the pallid light, the trees at the limit of the clearing were tall and dark and straight.

There was a slight dark shadow. Why should there be a slight dark shadow, when the circle of trees around the clearing were all massive single stem affairs? It moved too. Nothing else moved in the still, windless night. Without leaving the window, he stretched back with one hand and just reached the tip of the light control with an extended finger.

Light exploded like a bomb into the clearing. He had kept his eyes on the shadow and he saw a creature with brown fur, standing upright, open a simian mouth in a soundless scream and put long slender hands across great black liquid eyes like discs, before it leaped aside into deep shade. It was like something he had seen on an anthropology tape. Tarsier was it? A kind of lemur. But this was on a much bigger scale. It must have been all of five feet.

The music had cut off and Munro put his head through

the hatch. 'What's going on, Andy. Couldn't you live without seeing a tree again?'

'We're not alone any more. There's at least one king-size lemur out there. Looked harmless enough. Went off backwards like a blasted comet.'

'This'll stop Miranda taking walks in the wood.'

'Nothing's likely to do that. Praise be.'

No room on the ship would take the complement of fifteen specialists who assembled for the rare crew conference. Usually the decisions in space were made by the Captain, assisted, if he sought their advice, by the executive committee—Co-Pilot, Chief Navigator, Chief Power, Chief Communications plus any other specialist like the spatiographer. Even though the crew were well integrated as a team, there was a mystique about the detailed work of each section which drew them together in groups to face a crisis.

The space between the massive tripod legs was arranged to give a semi-circle of seats facing Anders and Fletcher. On the right Alvirez, Chas. Bennett and Susan Yardley—Navigation. In the centre Fergusson, Craig, Smith and Randle—Power. On the left Robertshaw, Munro, Ross, Ralph Myers and the two girls, Miranda and Karen.

Anders said, 'You'll all know the set up. I regret to have to tell you that there is almost no chance of being picked up. In the last hundred years there have been only three known landings here. I believe Dag has a plan he wants to talk about. It will be as new to me as to you, so let's hear it.'

Fletcher went straight into it without any cushioning preamble. 'That's the picture. No lift-off from this sylvan pad. But as you know, if you can pick your spot there is an optimum choice time-wise and place-wise for maximum help from the environment. On Pelorus that spot is the equatorial plateau. Time, not so important and we could wait for that. With its longer solar journey, Pelorus is only right for us for about six months in every two years. When dead right, I leave to Len to calculate.

'This is the key line. From the plateau we *could* lift off. It converts a clear "no" into a clear "yes"; with a margin I would take a chance on. Of course, we have to get there; and with the ship. We can't afford the power to play at being an Inter Continental Ballistic Missile, so we have to move it some other way. I believe we can do it.'

'Oh sure,' said Len Robertshaw. 'Nothing to it.' He looked up at the base of the towering ship. 'Which end will you take, Dag? I'll have the cone, it'll be easier to get hold of.'

Alvirez said, 'Wrong approach, Len. We're going to trap a few thousand of Craig's monster lemurs and train them to pull ropes. Pyramid stuff.'

'All right. Get over the funny patter and look at it this way.' Dag Fletcher leaned forward and bulldozed his points into their minds.

'We've come down in a natural lumber camp. You all saw how easily we cleared this site. These trees are a gift to work with. They have a density like Balsa wood. We can fell enough of these to make three massive cradles. Wheeled, if Chad can bend his mind to the engineering of it. Though even sledge runners might work. Then we need a gantry framework. Not too difficult. A mere scaffolding job. Break down the ship into its three basic modules and lower it on to the beds. Tow the lot with the half-track loading trolley and we're in business.'

There was a silence as the full implications unrolled in their minds.

Anders said slowly, 'It could work. At the other end, the wood from the cradles could make the gantry to reassemble the sections. In theory, at least, it could work. A slow job though. How far, Karen?'

'Give or take a few miles, eight hundred to the coast, two thousand three hundred at the most direct crossing and then another thousand to the equator. Incidentally, the coast lands would be tropical jungle. It might pay off to search along for some point where the Leucophanes mountains come down to the sea and go straight up.'

Fletcher said, 'Good girl. We'll consider that when we get there.'

'Steady with that, Dag. There's no decision taken yet,' interposed Anders. 'Have you anything else to add?'

Fletcher went on, 'Just one thing. By making the move, we have nothing at all to lose. In fact, even if we get holed up on the final stage, we simply have to make a life there instead of here. The climate is better there. Food supplies are easier. And we could always move back north until we found the right place.'

'If we were still alive, we could,' said Fergusson, temporarily infected by Robertshaw.

'No one can guarantee you life, Chad.'

Anders came in. 'I rule this a crew conference matter. The executive will follow a simple majority vote. This is no easy solution. It will be a slow job with a lot of hard work. And very great hazards. If we stayed here, we could cannibalise the ship and make some sort of settlement. As deep space personnel you have elected to be free of commitments which make it obligatory to return to any one centre. For my part, I would rather die here, in an attempt to get back, than live here. Any questions?'

Anders looked round impassively. 'There isn't much to ask about. It's a clear-cut decision. Take ten minutes and I'll put it to the vote.'

Alvirez got up and walked over to Fletcher. 'You've hit on a beauty there, Dag. I'm all for it. I can give you some help on design. Sailing is my second favourite pastime. If you want to set the mood for the replies, ask me first. Miranda will be good for a "yes" too—she hasn't said "no" for years. But from what I've seen, you'll get full backing.'

'Thanks, John. I hope you're right.'

Small groups talked it out. Anders knocked a tree trunk with a dry branch and the meeting gathered again.

'I'll ask Dag to make a formal record for the log. The question is, do we make a bid for the equator? An answer "Yes" says we do. An answer "No" says we stay here, but does not rule out consideration of any other scheme that might come up. All clear? Go ahead, Dag.'

Fletcher plugged in a small hand-set to a wandering lead, so that the record was fed back to the permanent log which always registered major policy decisions of executive or crew council.

'Day four. Position as recorded. 1115 hours. Crew Conference. Captain Anders presiding. Decision on attempt to move ship by land and sea to equatorial line for escape attempt. Communications staff, Miranda Dolon.'

Miranda's 'Yes' came back clear and forthright, followed by Myers and Ross without hesitation. Munro was lighting his pipe and took it out to say 'I don't believe it can be done; but "Yes" for me.'

Robertshaw's 'Yes' was without reservations and Dag moved on to the Power section. They would have the major part of the planning to do. Randle and Smith seemed indifferent but they were in with a 'Yes' for the ride. Craig and Chad Fergusson were positive with their agreement. Turning to the navigators, Dag was sure now of a unanimous decision. Susan Yardley sounded disappointed, but agreed. She had been looking forward to a settled life with open-hearth cookery. But she was a realist at heart. Bennett and Alvirez were enthusiastic. They knew Fletcher better than most people on the ship and what they knew they liked. If anyone could get the ship over its four thousand mile trek, they believed he could do it.

Dag put it on record: 'Unanimous affirmative.'

Anders looked round and smiled. He looked years younger.

'Thank you for that decision. As the oldest member of the group, it probably means more to me to get back than to any one of you. I believe we can do it. I'm sure this is the right choice. However long it takes, whatever it costs. The first move is to select and fell about a hundred trees and get a gantry built. Then we can move ahead on the cradles whilst the ship is being dismantled. We'll have a meal and make a token start today. From tomorrow—strict schedules. What do you reckon on time for the first phase, Dag?'

'It's early to say. I want us to pull out of this clearing in a month. But you never can tell.'

Like a whirling stroboscope, the tallest tree on the perimeter of the clearing plunged inwards towards the ship. Only the breaking of the pattern of light warned of its silent falling. Karen saw it from the corner of her eye and estimated in a flash where its tip would strike. Her mind screamed out a quick incisive command—'Dag, move left.' But the action was too quick for speech.

Where life often depended on reaction time, men and women of the Space Service were specially selected for abnormally quick reactions. There was no hesitation for Fletcher as he flung himself left and cannoned Anders off the seat beside him. The tip of the tree whipped down and shattered on the log. Even the slender growing point was four inches in diameter. It would have been certain death.

Nothing moved in the forest. Dark grey, straight tree trunks, olive green, blue-veined foliage, straw-coloured fern-like grass.

Miranda said uncertainly, 'I shall be glad to leave this place. There's something sinister about it. I've gone all goose pimples.'

'That's just exposure, dear,' said Susan Yardley, kindly. 'Let's move inside.'

Dag said, 'Thank you, Karen. It looks as though the decision would have been taken out of our hands.'

Anders was still brushing himself down.

'Record on the log that we break the seal on the armoury. Carry pistols wherever you go and don't go beyond the perimeter alone.'

Chad Fergusson said, 'At least that's one tree we don't have to fell.'

Karen was standing apart with Fletcher. She said, 'Don't thank me. I didn't say anything. I only wanted to.'

CHAPTER TWO

FROM the ports of the control cabin, Dag Fletcher looked down on the orderly activity in the extended clearing. Stacks of long regular trunks were forming at intervals across the full width. Just below the level of the ports, the first stage of a scaffolding ended in a platform. He made a log entry.

'Day 15. Steady progress. Gantry brought to one hundred feet. Logs ready to begin construction of cradles. Animal life returning to the area and supplies of fresh food now possible. Large troops of lemur-like simioids approach during the night. Behaviour is hostile; but no serious situation has developed.'

Down in the clearing, the caterpillar-tracked loading trolley came from between two timber stacks, towing a hundred foot tree trunk. Miranda had found her vocation as a tractor operator. Shoulder length hair rippling back like a honey blonde mane; the briefest shorts that could possibly be listed technically as clothing; skin tight amethyst blue shirt, the same colour as her eyes; she stood between the two half hoops at the rear of the small trolley and manœuvred it like a veteran. She swung in a tight circle and left the long log neatly in line with the centre stack, jumped down to free the drag link, then whipped back the way she had come.

Chad Fergusson was official Clerk of Works and had set up a cracking organisation. The only worry to Dag was the dependence they were, necessarily, putting on the small and vulnerable loading trolley. It was the universal chore horse and power plant. Except for work on the gantry, which was powered by the automatic hoists on the ship itself, every bit of towing, transporting and lifting was being carried out by the indefatigable half-track. Moreover it would be the towing unit for the whole caravan once they got under way and possibly the propellent for the barges when they were seaborne.

However, the trolleys were made for a lifetime of service without renewal of the self energising power component. Unless it were lost to them by falling down a hole, it was difficult to see what Miranda could do with it that would put it out of action.

The vibrator set had also given service. Its slender pointer had melted its way through the massive tree trunks in seconds. Then a vee, cut with a flourish in a very Latin way by Alvirez, and the tree was a push over.

In the absence of any other fastening device, the logs for the gantry had been notched in a simple dovetail, fitted home and then wedged. After a life-time spent manipulating the thin, light-weight, immensely strong metals used in space craft, it was incredibly clumsy to Chad and his engineers. But they enjoyed the rediscovery of old techniques. Building a gantry at the other end was going to be more of a problem. Without the ship itself standing there, it would be no picnic.

Karen swung herself through the hatch. 'I've got an idea, Dag, for working ahead on the route. Do we carry standard meteorology equipment?'

'Surely.'

'Top size balloons?'

'We'll dig it out. There should be two fifteen foot diameter affairs and one silvered blimp. The big one doubles as a signal reflector for certain difficulties on a no-atmosphere planet with a low radiation layer.'

'Could we have one take up an observer?'

'Just a minute, Karen. You're not proposing to go up with a weather balloon?'

'Why not? We'd get better than a hundred miles ahead. I've got a detailed plan for the first hundred miles from the scanner pictures as we came in to land. Beyond that we have a general idea; but no detail. We could get in real trouble, by not making the right detour. Waste weeks in back tracking. This way we could plan for a week's advance.'

Fletcher looked at her. Today the fine coppery hair was swathed and piled in a sophisticated style, which was almost a calculated gesture against the simplicities of the lumber camp. A plain lime green cheong sam followed every line and curve of her figure. Hanging precisely, between high, round breasts, a medallion on a thin platinum chain carried the initials K.E. in a monogram.

'You're too valuable a piece of equipment to send up in a weather balloon. But it certainly is an idea. I'll think about it.'

A booming gong note came from below.

'That's Susan ready with the mess of pottage. Let's go.'

Susan Yardley was in her element. She had persuaded Chad, not that it needed much persuasion, to practise his log construction technique on a long open-sided dining hall with a barbecue pit at one end. A fifteen foot refectory type table, built from three split logs, ran down the middle, with places for seven each side, At the top an elaborately carved chair, with arms, had been sculptured from one massive five foot stump. Alvirez was enjoying himself with the vibrator. Eleven simple chairs with straight backs were notched out of solid trunks. The other three, which he presented to the girls, were as elaborate as the one for Anders, but patterned heavily with a heart motif.

The gong brought everyone in to watch Susan heave a young antelope on to a serving table and dissect it into joints with a small cell-powered vibrator. Hydroponic tanks on the ship had produced green vegetables. Fruit came from bushes in the forest. Banana-like in shape; thick sectioned skin, firm blue flesh and pear flavoured. Checked by Ralph Myers, who doubled as biologist, it had become very popular.

Ched produced a sketch for the leading cradle.

'Twenty-six feet long' he pointed out, 'gives a protective overlap of one foot for the cone tip. Clinker built, continuous shell of planks under the module with axles and eight solid wheels. Bearings of infrangom. We shall have to sacrifice the spare combustion chamber lining.'

'What sort of weight?' asked Dag.

'The whole ship is two hundred and forty tons dead weight. This section takes care of about fifty tons. We shall have to mount it so that the vacuum seal hatches are accessible. It carries the hydroponic tanks.'

'How about the rest?'

'Control module, sixty feet and one hundred and ten tons. That's the headache. Over difficult country we shall have to move the sections one at a time. Once in the water it'll be plain sailing to coin a phrase.'

'And the power pack?'

'We can shorten that by dismantling the tripod. That will leave about sixty feet again and the best of ninety tons.'

'But you think you can beat it?'

'I'm sure we can make the cradles and move out from here. Then it's your problem.'

'Yes. It's not going to be easy to choose a practicable route. Karen's come up with an idea using a weather balloon. Can you rig an undercarriage to take an observer?'

'I'll put Lew Randle on it this afternoon.'

'Final thing, Chad. How long before we can move. This dry spell won't last for ever and I don't fancy our chances of moving in mud.'

'Within four weeks.'

Chad gave his attention to a two pound steak. Don Munro started up a digesting tune on his squeeze box. Miranda found the chair on her right was still empty, 'Where's Alec; he said he was following me in?'

The clear, rather petulant soprano hit a lull in the general clatter and Anders looked round the group. 'Where was he working?'

Trees were being felled in a line from the clearing, so that the caravan could move off down a ready made avenue.

'He was down at the end of the road.' Miranda appealed to Smith. 'You saw him, Ven.'

'Probably he's back in the ship. Keep a piece hot for him, Susan.'

'And there's an opportunity for a witty line,' said Alvirez. 'However, Miranda, I wouldn't like your close friend to miss his dinner. I, myself, personally, will go and find him.'

Conversation renewed itself. Susan was congratulated. Munro sidled into another of his composite tunes. Dag could see Alvirez disappearing on the hoist into the ship. He saw him come out alone, walk over to the loading trolley and take it at speed down the avenue.

It was unlike Alec to miss a meal and unlike him to stay away from Miranda for so long. Dag left the table and went out to the beginning of the avenue. He saw Alvirez, at the far end where the trees still blocked the way, spin the trolley on its tracks and start back. He noticed for the first time that there was silence in the forest again. After the first few days, when wild life had been scared away by the blazing inferno created by the landing ship, there had been a gradual return to full scale orchestration of forest noises. Birds particularly, with occasional high pitched chatterings and coyote-like howls. Now it was quite still.

Alvirez spun to a broadside stop beside him. 'Nothing down there. I gave him a call. He surely wouldn't go wandering off on his own at this time of day?'

'Miranda spoke to him about twenty minutes ago and he knew it was nearly time to break.'

'Have you noticed anything?'

'The silence?'

'What do you make of it?'

'Could happen regularly at this time—a sort of natural siesta. Can't say I've registered it before though.'

'What's the next move then?'

'We'll give him another fifteen minutes and that'll give everyone a rest. Then we'll have to search around.'

'Check.'

The meal ended with a detectable drop in the conversation level. People were uneasily skating round the subject of what could have happened to Alec. Nobody had seen anything to report during the morning. Anders organised four parties to search. They reported after an hour that there was no trace.

Len Robertshaw slapped his forehead with the palm of his hand.

'This simple life is addling my brain. We should all stop wandering about and do a grid search on the scanner. Miranda, be a good girl and run down a square mile centred on the ship. Break it into squares on a twenty yard base line. That should show up a rabbit.'

In addition to more obvious qualifications, Miranda had an instinct for communications work which made her a key figure in that section. Thirty minutes later she reported on the link to the mess hall. 'No good I'm afraid. There's no movement of anything at all in this immediate area.' She sounded near to tears.

Anders said, 'Thanks, Miranda. Leave it at that. If he can get back, I'm sure he will do so. If he can't, we might have one more reason for getting out of here as quickly as we can. Back to work. Don't go out of sight. Keep in pairs. Can we afford a continuous watch on the scanner, Dag?'

'Not really. Neither in manpower nor fuel. Except at night, of course.'

'All right then. Come on, snap into it.'

Chad worked with a concentrated anger at the top stage of the gantry, swinging up the relatively light, but clumsy, trunks and clouting in wedges as if they were personal enemies. There were enough hazards in space to end a man, without going out in a forest on a lumber operation. There was no fitness in it. With an effort of will, he brought his mind to total concentration on the problems in front of him. He built up four immense props, cross girdered and stayed and with bonus strength to sway down the top section of the ship.

Fletcher came up for instructions. He and Alvirez were working on the wheels. 'Can you take a look at these bearings, Chad?'

Strips of combustion chamber lining made from infrangom—a relatively new metal used in space craft—had been shaped to make collars for the centres of the solid wooden wheels. Running on a similar strip bound on the stub axle, this made a bearing which would not wear at all. 'Yes, that looks all right. Pack it with fat and it should give very little friction. How many have you made?'

'Eight.'

'Fine. We might get away with six on the first stage. That means another fourteen and then turn your inventive minds to drag links.'

They worked a long afternoon session. Mostly in silence. A space crew was special in its relationships. Much psychological data was gathered and processed when a crew was selected. It was no hit or miss business. The long months in space would soon show up any serious disharmony and they were chosen people, each with a niche, each with an individual contribution to make to the success of the mission. *Interstellar Two-Five* was a good ship. Well integrated. Each one felt personally involved.

Fletcher found Anders working on the planking of the first cradle. 'What do you make of it, Pete?'

'It doesn't change anything. We still have to work your plan as long as there are enough people to make sense of it.'

'That's about it. But some hostile agency must be involved. And if it were powerful enough, it would strike at once and finish the job. Since it doesn't do that, it must believe it can't do it. In that case, extra caution on our side should be enough.'

'That hangs together.'

'But we can't afford to lose another one. The score could have been two down. Even at the risk of slowing up the job, we must brief personnel on security. Operate in twos. Keep in sight of other groups. I can't fathom where the danger comes from. On the face of it, Craig's lemur doesn't look a likely candidate. He described a night creature. Though the lights we fixed up would have startled anyone of normal vision. But where do they go?'

'Tarsiers were embryo brains. They only lacked size to take over the evolutionary line. They could be very well developed here. Extrasensory perception even.'

'That would explain a lot. We can only press ahead for an early move out.'

'I'd agree with that. We can begin to assemble this first cradle tomorrow and then Chad can swing down the first section. Living in the ship as we move isn't going to be too bad. Now, for God's sake, Dag, shut up and let me get on.'

Anders was enjoying the manual labour. After a lifetime manipulating mathematical imponderables and setting his life on the hair thread of a computer course, it was a relief to work with something tangible that took shape under his hands.

Jointed and pegged like the gantry, it was expected that the logs would expand in water and make a water-tight hull. Not that it would matter as far as the ship was concerned. Once the vacuum seal hatches were closed, it could not sink, but it had to be navigated. And the wooden shell would be a protective sheath against damage.

Dag understood how Anders was feeling and went back to Alvirez. Two more completed bearings showed that no time was being wasted. 'I'll carry on there, John. Will you go and see how Karen is making out with the weather balloon. No need to say I don't want her to go up in it. You make sure she doesn't.'

'That's a change for the better. But softly, do I see a fine Italian hand at work? Do you want me to face the first anger of a thwarted feminist?'

'That I didn't think of. But now you mention it, it's a very good idea. I'm sure you'll be able to put it so that she thinks she's doing you a real favour.'

Karen and Lew Randle were putting the finishing touches to a very basic aircraft when Alvirez arrived. Partly inflated, one of the fifteen foot weather balloons was tethered to the open gable end of the dining-hall. A few parachute packs were carried, to clip on to space suits as a safety measure for repair crews working on grounded ships. The biggest craft stood two hundred and fifty feet on their tripods and a quick-acting automatic chute was a reasonable precaution. Particularly since some absent minded types, used to extravehicular activity in deep space, tended to fend off and expected to float. Randle had spliced the harness of one on to the existing network of the balloon and the belt and shoulder gear now swung ten feet below the release valve.

'And who draws this lucky number?' said Alvirez. 'Who does the aerial ballet in the sunshine, whilst the horny-handed toilers burn out their brief lives in this satanic mill?'

'Me.'

'Strictly, that should be "I do". But no doubt you have your reasons for avoiding that. When's the trial flight?'

'Now.'

'What about it, Lew, is it a good risk?'

'Very safe. Operator in a suit with a parachute pack. Shouldn't be any trouble. Karen doesn't know it yet, but I'll try it out first.'

'Fine, that takes care of my problem.'

Randle completed the job by fixing the free end of a two hundred and fifty foot coil of thin nylon cable to the cordage, other coils could be added by snapping on to the patent fastener which ended each length. The axle of the reel slotted into clips on the rear rail of the loading trolley, which Miranda was bringing into the clearing with her last log of the afternoon. Randle unhitched the balloon and towed it across.

'Stay where you are, Miranda, we might need some ballast.'

He clipped in the reel and wound down the balloon to give it its extra boost of gas. Then he knocked free the pawl. It rose rapidly to fifty feet, where he held it with the friction brake. The empty harness dangled free; plumb centre.

'I'll be a few minutes getting into a suit. Wind it down with the power take off, Karen, will you?'

Randle walked away before he could get the wrong answer, and Alvirez said, 'Lew will be a great man. I'll tell Anders you're ready for a trial.' As he went off to find the Captain, Karen said, 'Well to hell with all that for a start. Give me a hand, Miranda. This is my idea and I'm going to work it out.'

'Surely,' there was more animation in the voice than at any time since the discovery of Alec's disappearance. 'I've got my zip suit somewhere about. You'll need something up there.'

Karen fed power to the spindle and the balloon homed on to the trolley until the harness was swinging at chest height. Miranda was back with her dazzling lime green track-suit and helped Karen to put it on. It was not quite so dramatically filled as by its owner; but it would make all the difference comfort wise.

Karen said as she pulled in the last harness strap, 'Send

me up to two hundred feet. Then watch my hands. One hand raised and I want in. Both hands raised and I want another fifty feet up.'

'Check.'

Miranda released the pawl and the balloon began a steady rise. Slower this time, but fast enough.

The great cinnamon ball of the sun was low in the sky. There was no breeze. It was mildly warm at twenty-one degrees Centigrade. Karen rose level with the still tree tops and then climbed on. Past the soaring slender aerial at the tip of the cone. She looked down on the blue green tide of foliage and beyond, to where it gradually tapered out into rolling grassland and bush in a long spread to the horizon. This would certainly do the trick. As the photographs and scanner pictures had already made clear, there was no immediate problem for a route. It was straight out on a compass direction, as the ancient settlers in South Africa were believed to have trekked in primitive waggons.

She was glad of the zip suit. At two hundred feet there was a stop and she signalled to go to two fifty and then to three hundred. A flock of white birds broke out from the trees and wheeled suddenly against the disc of the sun as if startled by something below them. Far out on the plain, groups of dots appeared to move. Could be animal herds. Troops of lemurs.

The balloon began to haul in and she looked down. Miranda had been joined by several others. Dag Fletcher appeared to be working the reel. Lew was there in full regalia. As she touched down, she began—'It works very well. Used every day, we should avoid any serious routing problems. . . .'

Dag Fletcher was looking at her with a cold glare that stopped her dead. The habits of six years in military service, three of them in command of his own ship, had surfaced over the milder manners of a civilian executive. She began to doubt the wisdom of her action.

'When I said you were too valuable to test out this device

yourself, I meant just that. Will you remember that you have a special function on this executive, which no one else can fulfil. I do not expect to have to spell out every simple message to senior personnel. Get out of that harness and get into a space-suit. Send Lew up with the balloon and use the intercom as a link. Then report.'

To her own annoyance, Karen found that she was automatically doing as she was told. It was many years since she had been told so directly what to do. It was a bitter pill to take. More so, since a balanced judgment, way back in her mind, told her that he was right and only a strict rule of law could keep an isolated party, like their own, in being as an effective unit. But it was sweetened to some extent by the fact that she was aware of what was also in his mind. Even whilst he was tearing off his strip; at another level, he was admiring her enterprise and more than admiring her physically. She said, 'It will be a clumsy arrangement if I have to map a route from second-hand information. I want to see the ground with my own eyes.'

'That may be so. I want the safety of the method established first. If you go up again you will be properly equipped and directed.'

In spite of the long afternoon's work, there was no lessening of the impact of the loss of Alec Ross when they gathered again in the dining hall. Myers had moved out the empty chair, but the big question mark was there.

Anders said, 'We have to accept the fact that Alec has met some kind of end. He was a good spaceman. Before we leave this place we will make a memorial for him.'

Fletcher added, 'It becomes more important to take the watch duties seriously. Into the ship at dusk and no movement outside until daylight.'

Chad Fergusson said, 'Tomorrow you can work in the clearing. We have enough timber to make a start on the big cradles. Dan will run a heat hose down from the ship and we can soften up the trunks and mould them. Operation Ark. Use the power-assisted suit as a lifting aid.'

'Who plays Father Christmas in that?' asked Susan.

The power-assisted suit was a piece of little-used apparatus, carried as a regulation item for fire fighting or difficult rescue jobs. The operator was in a miniature, independent excursion module. Arms and legs were articulated tubular metal with great power and strength. Initial moves by the wearer were copied and carried out by the robot mechanism. It was, to all intents and purposes, a close control robot. It would be an ideal instrument for construction. Elephant strength, man brained.

'I'll do it'—said Miranda unexpectedly.

Chad looked at her. In spite of appearances, she was a very sensitive operator of mechanical gadgets. Perhaps, in some obscure way, it was to be a sort of gesture for Alec. The local equivalent of a temporary retreat to a nunnery. Certainly nothing could be more impersonal than the power suit.

'All right, Miranda. I'm sure you'll be a great help.'

In the days that followed, this was proved to be a good choice. Block and tackle, mounted on the gantry, swung down the top section of the ship and Miranda steadied it into its prepared chocks on the leading cradle. Heated planks were moulded and held and pegged into place. The three stage caravan grew.

Day twenty-eight saw the bedding-in of the power module.

'What's the drill for the final drive, Chad? Are you using the half-track by itself or mounting it on the first stage?'

'To pull this lot, it needs some weight on its tracks. I have an idea to make a niche for it under the rear axle. When we get to float, we can mount rocket tubes for direct thrust into the water. Another day, Dag, and the caravan is all yours and I can put my feet up.'

The three stages were lined up across the clearing with the leading vehicle pointing down the avenue. A sufficient path had been cleared to take them out of the wood on to open ground. On the left of the column the empty gantry stood, stripped of usable tackle. The power suit was clearing up the remnants of a timber stack which lay across the path of the caravan. Suddenly it hit itself violently across the bottom half of its solid cowl with a metallic clank that could be heard across the clearing. As Dag looked up and saw the tail of the action, it pitched forward. He was running towards it when it fell across the logs and lay still.

Visible in the gap made by the movement of the last log; lying on his face, left arm flung forward, green striped shirt torn away from the neck, showing the back of a gold identity chain, Alec Ross was found.

It took three men to lift the power suit clear. Then Susan and Karen began to ease off the clips and pressure seals to dig Miranda out. After the involuntary movement of putting a hand up to her mouth, magnified a hundredfold by the power mechanism, she had locked the controls by fainting with hands clenched on the palm buttons of the gauntlets.

Fletcher said, 'Break out one of the disposal sacks, Lew. We'll get him out of here before Miranda comes round. Get Myers along to have a look at him.'

Randle brought back the seven foot plastic sack rolled in its tiny container and zipped it out. They opened the mouth and put him in, feet first. Before sealing the end, Dag slipped off the chain from the neck. Myers arrived and went straight to the same site. He felt gently round the area of the throat to the top of the spine. Then it was done, and the opaque plastic concealed the body.

'How did he die?' asked Anders.

Myers said, 'Broken neck. Not here, of course. He must have been put under the stack later.'

Fletcher said, 'But not much later. Probably sometime during that night. That would check; because after that, the log stack grew pretty high. So much for our unsleeping eyes.'

'Who was on duty that night?'

'I'd have to check the log to be sure. As far as I remember, I was on myself until 2700 hours. Then Smith came on. He would do a four hour stint until 0300. After that, I don't know.'

Anders changed the subject.

'We can't take him along.'

Sometimes, where it was a known wish that a spaceman wanted to be returned to Earth after death, he was carried back. The long trek ahead would be transformed into a cortège.

'No. He stays here. The gantry can be a funeral pyre. To-night he will lie on the top platform under guard.'

Ready to leave, Dag swung himself up on the leading waggon. Kindling at the base of the gantry began to flame. All the remaining timber had been stacked between the supports. He called down to Chad Fergusson, who had improvised remote controls for the invisible loading trolley, 'Let her roll, Chad.'

Anders, Fletcher, Fergusson, Smith and Karen Evander travelled with the cone; Alvirez, Craig, Robertshaw, Myers and Miranda Dolon were with the long centre section and Bennett, Randle, Munro and Susan Yardley brought up the rear.

As the tracks bit and the wheels began a slow turn, Miranda jumped down from a high perch on the command module. She stumbled, recovered, then ran back to the blazing pyramid. They had all felt a sense of occasion in leaving the clearing and she was wearing her most effective ceremonial tabard. A flash of green and bronze and honey blonde hair. She stripped a heavy jade bracelet from a golden brown arm and threw it into the spiralling flames. Then back without a pause, running beside the lumbering cart. Alvirez and Craig leaned down to lift her up and in with a swing.

At a walking pace, the three-stage caravan rocked down the

cleared lane and pulled out into open country. The ground here was flecked with outcrops of blue stone. Sparse grass and occasional belts of low bush. Undulating. Chad pushed up the speed to ten miles an hour. They could average a hundred miles a day at this rate.

Chad registered that even in the open, there was a curious flicker effect as if they were moving through varying intensities of light. It was impossible to detect any variation in the bland, featureless, cinnamon sky. He closed his eyes. It was the same. Every ten yards or so. Like moving through invisible barriers of fine gauze.

Cresting the second slow rise, Anders signalled down for a halt and they looked back. A thick column of smoke rose vertically over the clearing, tinged with flame just above tree-top level. Birds were wheeling and settling uncertainly. A troop of about twenty lemurs broke cover from the edge of the wood and then stood facing the distant convoy. There was some doubt whether they had been responsible for Alec's death. Getting the body back into the clearing was just too clever for anybody's comfort. The creatures stood motionless for about a minute. Then they wheeled in unison and disappeared into the shelter of the trees.

Alvirez stood with an arm round Miranda's shoulders. 'To coin a phrase—a journey of a thousand miles begins with one steppe.'

He got the full treatment of a very warm smile at close quarters. 'You are being nice to me, John. Help me climb through this hatch. I want to change into something more comfortable.'

As he made a stirrup with joined hands and lifted her to reach the rim of the entry port, Alvirez reflected that there was something about the back of the knees of a girl as pretty as Miranda, which had a very unsettling effect on him. What was so special about that tiny area though?

Quite suddenly, he had the curious sensation of being in

a dual role. He was not only looking appreciatively at Miranda's perfectly modelled legs, he was also on the other side of the fence. He was inside Miranda's mind which had the knowledge of being looked at. He was aware of an uncomplicated pleasure in exciting admiration. He was aware of what it was like to *be* Miranda. He recognised, with a sense of revelation, that there was that basic sweetness in her disposition which every man hoped to find in a woman, and seldom, if ever, did. Then the convoy began to move and he was outside again. He gave it up and looked back. Only the spreading pall of black smoke remained visible.

Acting on impulse, he reached up and grasped the hatch coaming. With a powerful heave, he hoisted himself on to the rim and then reached up to a ceiling grab and swung himself inside. Miranda had gone ahead; but there was a faint trace of her perfume. As he went down the corridor, Chad Fergusson coaxed his speed back to ten miles an hour and the cradle began to sway with a boat's motion. 'Nature,' he said wisely to himself, 'abhors a vacuum.'

CHAPTER THREE

KAREN EVANDER'S voice, precise and efficient on the intercom, announced that she had seen enough. Smith fed power to the reel and brought the observer balloon in at a run. She came down at the rear of the cone section, unclipped the harness and climbed down into the triangular laager.

Each of the last six nights had been the same. At the end of the day's run, Smith or Fergusson, whichever one was finishing a duty spell, swung the leading section until the trailers came round in a nose to tail triangle. Then Karen went up to three hundred feet, swinging below the weather balloon. With compass, recording binoculars, which registered selected views on micro film, and a prepared sketch, she plotted out a detailed route for the next day's travel. It had paid off with few errors—and those few unavoidable. As when a blind foldback in the ground, invisible from above, had concealed a dried-out gulley which had to be bridged. That had taken half a day of very dicey manœuvring and some nice calculations of stresses by the engineers. But some days had given a bonus mileage and they were well on schedule within two hundred miles of the coast.

She hinged back the helmet and the flurry of local sound came in, instead of the piped precision of the intercom. In the twenty minutes of detailed observation, a lot had happened at ground level. They had moved significantly farther south in the last two hundred miles and it was pleasantly warm. So meals were outdoors and a table had been set up. A shallow trench had been taken out and a fire was blazing

42

in it. Susan had worked on Munro and Lew Randle until they were dedicated cook orderlies. Strips of meat rolled on skewers were spitting fat into the flames. All very palæolithic.

She methodically eased out the pressure seals and worked out of her suit. It was a five minute chore in itself. She carried it over her arm to the clear space at the rear of the waggon and dumped it inside. It looked as though dinner would be some time yet; so there was time to pull the notes into presentable shape, before the executive conference which was held every night to fix the details of the next day's moves. She climbed into the command module to make use of the chart spread.

Anders and Dag Fletcher, from the space beside the chocks, which held the tip of the cone, looked out at the heavy grey blur on the horizon. Anders said, 'So far so good. We've made remarkable time. Things are going too well.'

'It can't be too smooth for me. But there must be snags before we hit the coast. Any forest belt would slow us to a crawl. Animal life, too, is bound to increase. There's really very little known about Pelorus. It wouldn't surprise me at all to find hominids or even early cultures. I'd like to know what Karen makes of that line over there. She's being on the formal side with me just now, so I save my queries for the briefing session.'

The pinkish light of Pelorus began to thicken into the long dusk as Dan Munro made a theme and variations on a cookhouse call. They were all pleased with the progress they had made and morale was high. Even Robertshaw conceded that the statistical odds against making out were reducing.

'Instead of a million to one against—it's down to a hundred thousand to one against—which is considerable improvement.'

'Thank you very much, Len,' said Miranda. 'You are a comfort. It's nice to know we're trekking through this Gobi for the good it does us, and without any ulterior motive— like going home.'

'Home is where you make it,' put in Alvirez sententiously.

'Make what?'

'Surely you know?'

The executive conference met in the control cabin. With the ship on its side, the gymbal mountings had swung to bring couches and table horizontal, but negotiating the corridor and hatch under full gravity still seemed unusual. Karen had pencilled in a route on a large scale chart.

'By tomorrow night we should be in sight of the sea. My horizon even at three hundred feet was limited by the hills; but there looked to be nothing out of the way about them. There's a gradual rise from about twenty miles on and then it builds up to a range of low hills. Extends left and right without a break. Unless you want to try a detour—and there's nothing to suggest that it would be any good—we might just as well try to cross in a direct line. There is a saddle between two peaks which is a natural choice. This I cannot say with certainty; but there could be organised life in the area. There is regularity of ground features which might be earthworks. Here's the best picture I got.'

Karen flipped out a microfilm capsule which Alvirez obligingly set up in the ancillary feed to the main scanner screen. The grey blur of the horizon resolved itself into the distant foothills. Certainly there were regular patches of darker ground which seemed to follow the contour of the hills.

'That could be terracing,' said Anders slowly. 'There's very little depth of soil. Soil conservation would follow a plan like that.'

'I believe you're right, Pete,' said Fletcher. 'In which case the line given by Karen is the only possible one to follow. We can only hope we don't strike a terrace further in that comes right across. I don't fancy lifting this lot up the side of a wall.'

'That's not the only thing, Dag,' put in Robertshaw. 'Terracing means cultivation and that means people. They could have seen us already. Will they understand about us being gentle and peaceful travellers, just looking for a place to build a spaceship. It sounds a bit thin.'

'That we can only sort out when we get there. But to be on the safe side, we should get into space gear after the mid-day halt tomorrow. If it doesn't give complete protection, it at least has a sobering effect on primitives who see it for the first time.'

Anders said, 'Very well, we'll do that and follow the line as planned. Thank you again, Karen. One thing before we go. We've been supplementing the food stocks fairly well, but how do we go on food and water?'

'Food is no problem.' Chad regarded supply as a sub-responsibility of the power group. 'And water is no problem with the ship in full working order. But we are relying just now on the water by-product of the energy cells and this is low. Nothing to spare at all. Maybe we shall come across some natural supplies in the hills.'

'I can find a use for more energy,' said Dag. 'I want the lighting doubled round the laager. This power shutdown leaves us very vulnerable.' Accustomed to the devastating force of a corvette, he was very conscious that they were out on a limb if it came to any kind of trouble.

'That you can have,' said Chad, 'and a bonus wash for every man, woman and child after breakfast.'

Making a start an hour after dawn, they were near enough to see more detail at the mid-day halt. There was no doubt about it. The long continuous lines, like contours on a relief map, were some kind of terracing. Dag put on a suit and went up with the balloon. From above, the flat bands of cultivated land were clear to see. Probably not more than twenty paces in depth, they ran left and right as far as the hills could be seen. This would argue some considerable settlements or cave dwellings and some development beyond the very earliest stages of human life. Well, they were not anthropologists, he would settle for getting through without hindrance. There was an argument for giving ships like *Two-Five* some protective armament. In this situation, even one heavy calibre Laser would have seen them through.

Two hours later, the ground began to rise and the whine of the trolley motor deepened a tone as it took the extra load. In front of them, a gentle slope led forward, between over-lapping spurs of more steeply climbing ground. Clearly visible, terracing began about two miles further on. Packed earth and irregular shaped stones had been formed into retaining walls. If it was continuous across the whole frontage, they might just as well turn back and begin an indefinite detour.

Chad swung them round the first spur. More rising ground and another obscuring fold ahead. 'Keep it going. We'll just have to keep our fingers crossed.'

They ground round a tight right-hand bend with the wheels biting into both sides of the shale and scree in the narrowing valley bottom. A long shallow trough lay ahead ending with another blind spur and a tangle of logs. Dag snatched up his glasses and took a close look. There were no trees about. The logs were a calculated obstacle. In fact they were organised to give a defensive position. But there was nothing to be gained by turning yet. 'Slowly, Chad,' he said.

The caravan went ahead at a walking pace until the tree barrier was fifty yards ahead. 'Hold it there.'

Susan Yardley shouted from the rear trailer.

'Avalanche!'

From the top of the cone section, Dag looked back to see boulders and scree from both flanks pour in to fill the narrow opening through which they had come. There was no doubt about it, they were up against a human type adversary capable of planning ahead.

'It's no good hanging about to see what develops. Be ready to get inside and seal up if there's a rush. I'll get into the power suit and take a look at that lot.' He swung himself off the cone and made the command module at a run and disappeared inside. Anders and Fergusson snapped down helmet seals and took out the small Laser pistols which formed the only armoury of civilian ships. After the last stone had found zero momentum, there was silence. A dust cloud hung in the air over the pass and began to drift down towards them. The space-suits would be useful in more than one way.

Fletcher went forward at a steady walk. The massive suit had a robot atmosphere about it which communicated to the wearer. Completely closed down, vision was indirect by rotating prisms set in a heavily armoured semisphere on top of the helmet dome. He reached the barrier and found that it rose several feet above the eight foot level of his head. He gripped a horizontal beam in the centre of the mass and began a slow, experimental push. The power suit developed well over two thousand horse power and something had to go.

Creaking and splintering the mixed barrier of bushes and small trees began to bend inwards under the strain, then it suddenly gave way and Dag stumbled forward through a ragged gap.

Whoever had built it had not waited to see what would happen. There was no living thing in sight. The pass wound on to another masking spur. One thing was clear. They would have to keep moving. Any camp here would be a sitting target for an attack from the hillsides. They were set up like pins in a bowling alley.

He turned back to the barrier and methodically cleared the centre to a width of twenty feet. Then he called Fergusson on his intercom. Since they were all on the intercom link, he used group procedure with their number identifications. In this hierarchical system, Anders, he and Fergusson were 1; 2; 3. It ranged down the sections to Miranda as a sultry 15.

'Two to three.'

'Three. Carry on.'

'Bring it along slowly. I'll walk ahead. Out.'

Anders came in. 'One to two. Any sign of life?'

The convoy began to grind forward. Dag's reply was altered as he framed it, by a succession of blows on his helmet dome. It was like being struck by padded hammers. The ringing metallic clangs, which came through the audio set, seemed quite unconnected with the events. He spun the scanner eye. Higher up the hillside, far ahead to left and right, there was movement and then stillness again. At his feet were a number of round pebbles about the size of hen's eggs. Not bad marksmanship for that distance. 'Two to one. There is some kind of life about. Don't go bareheaded. Slingshot experts. Suggest we keep going until we get through. Over.'

'One to group. You heard that. Keep buttoned up. One to two. I agree, we'll halt at the other side. Out.'

Whatever was hovering about on their flanks was very unwilling to risk a confrontation. The clumsy trailers ploughed forward, keeping about ten yards behind the leading figure. Pebble shots were thudding at the timbers and gonging like drum hammers on the metal shell of the ship. There was not much immediate danger; though a lucky shot might do damage. Statistically, it was only a matter of enough shots before the lucky one turned up. They rounded another spur and the saddle opened out in more gradual slopes for the next few miles. Way ahead, it narrowed again; but any problems there could wait until they arrived.

'Six to two. I believe I can identify figures on the hillside' —Karen's voice was cool and efficient. 'Heavily camouflaged. They're in sight all the time; but stay motionless. Look closely at the edges of the stone patches.'

Dotted about the hillsides were discolourations which had the appearance of stony outcrops. The predominant colour of the ground was blue-grey. These lighter patches of grey had irregular blue-grey markings and melted into the general background.

Dag sent up an antenna and focussed on one with his

private scanner. It was quite true. They were not part of the ground. There was a distinct shadow line. To avoid uniformity they were in groups of different sizes, but each group on close inspection split down into a basic unit about two feet by four feet six. That meant a smallish man—possibly under five feet in height, crouched under a covering cloak carefully designed to match the texture of the hillside.

'Two to six, quite right. I see them now. There must be hundreds of them. Thank you, Karen. Two to one. It doesn't make any difference, we can only go on as far as we can.'

'Check.'

Now that they knew what to look for it was easier to spot the movements. One of the members of a group would rise to knee height, sling a shot and drop down again. All in a split second and timed to coincide with a moment when no one was looking directly that way. It was dovetailed perfectly, as if each one were directed in turn by some well-placed observer. The camouflage was very good and no precise picture could be built up. Karen focussed her camera binoculars on one group and hoped for the best. If the ship's control room had been operational, it would have been easy to get a tracking device beamed on to them. But this would do very well, if one of them moved. She casually turned her head away from the glasses; but kept them ranging on the target. Out of the tail of her eye, she saw the movement she had been waiting for, and hoped that it was registered on film.

Meanwhile they had reached the narrower part of the pass. Fletcher went on, still climbing. The trolley motor hit a new growling low and the trailers pulled slowly forward. Any narrower and they would have an engineering job to clear out part of the hillside. Terrace walls came down low on either side. It was easy to see the construction. Mortarless walls of irregular sized stones with drainage channels left. Very impressive.

Then they were at the top. The way down was similar to

the way they had come as far as could be seen. Chad crested the summit with the leading section and went on. The long middle section straddled the hummock and its underbelly hit the ground. Where this had happened on more open country, it had been easy enough to manœuvre it off. Here they were cramped for space. The logs furrowed in and the trolley began to develop enough torque to tear itself loose altogether. Chad throttled back and called up Anders: 'Three to one. This is going to be an all hands job.'

Dag was already coming back. He cut in with, 'Two to one. We'll need to excavate. It's a matter of taking the top off the hillock. Pass out the vibrator.'

'One to two. Check. One to thirteen. Dig out the vibrator and pass it forward.'

Lew Randle heaved open the pressure hatch of the power module and climbed in. Bennett, Munro and Susan Yardley were already travelling inside and had heard the transmission. As Randle came through, Bennett said, 'Seven to thirteen. Here you are, Lew boy. Catch hold. I'm right behind you.'

Between them they carried the vibrator gear out to where Dag was crawling under the low overhang of the middle waggon. He took the two-foot long vibrator needle and probed ahead.

'Two to thirteen. Switch in some power.'

The needle sliced through the earth and rock. He carved out cubic foot blocks and brushed them back as if they had been crumbs. Bennett and Randle cleared them more slowly to either side.

Karen Evander's voice came through, even and unhurried.

'Six to one. We may be in for a rush. They're nearer all round.'

Miranda had never fully accepted the discipline of group procedure on the intercom. In fact it could often be dispensed with. But, in stressed situations, it was a guarantee of precedence and avoided confusion of voices on the common link.

Her voice, anyway, was unmistakable as she said. 'What we need, Dan, is some basic "Last Post" music on the amplifiers.'

'Anything to oblige a lady.'

'Plug yourself on the direct link to control and I'll fix it up.'

Dan Munro was never very far from his squeeze box. Seconds later, before Anders had made up his mind whether or not to put in a veto, a clear, shrill trumpet of sound was echoing round the hillsides. Every melancholy, forlorn cadence that could be brought together to make the quintessence of them all was compounded in it. Then it shaded off into a pastiche of a wailing bagpipe lament.

The sound itself was startling, but the visual effect was remarkable. It was as if a bomb had fallen in the valley. Movement of hundreds of the camouflaged figures gave the impression of a landslide in reverse. The precision and timing of their movements broke down completely. The camouflage pattern was no longer maintained. Beneath the music a quiet singing of voices like a sighing wind. Then the hillsides were bare.

Miranda sounded very pleased. 'You really are clever, Dan. Come up into the control room and then I can get all the subtle harmonics.'

Anders came in.

'One to fifteen. Thank you, Miranda. Now do me a favour and keep off the air for the next ten minutes. One to two. What progress?'

Fletcher had cut back into the mount until he was at the point of balance. The whole heavy trailer was ready to sway forward. 'Two to one. Any minute now. I'm coming from under. What's going on?'

'Dan played them some music and they all went home.'

'I'm not surprised.'

He crawled out and called Fergusson. 'Two to three. Take her along slowly, Chad.'

The lead vehicle crept ahead and the long middle section

tipped forward. They were in business again. In spite of its weight, the shorter rear section managed the hazard without much difficulty and Dan switched to a 'Circus comes to Town' medley.

They went on. More narrow defiles. Another rising section and this time, by getting up steam and bashing at it, Chad scraped through the crest without a halt. Then the swaying descent again. The slow twilight gathered in the hills. Fletcher still strode ahead like a monstrous figure of doom. He called back for maximum light. Miranda suggested that he ought to have a red flag. They went on. Dan Munro said, 'Nine to anybody at all. What about a pint for the man at the piano?'

Miranda said, 'That's all right, Dan. I've recorded the programme; any time you like we'll go over to a repeat.'

'Thank you very much. How long were you going to let me go on before you revealed that little secret?'

'I thought you were enjoying yourself.'

They went on in violet darkness with a pale moon rising to begin its racing trek in an arc behind them. The planet Talos showed as a large bright red star. A very distant objective. The pass widened and the slope down was almost negligible, when Fletcher stopped and let the convoy come up to him.

'Two to one. We seem to be out of the hills. This would be all right for a camp.'

'One to group. Halt. Laager here. Report in to control room. Out.'

Smith was driving and brought the trailers round into a meticulous triangle. Accustomed to long hours of duty as they were, it was a more than welcome decision. Susan had managed to circulate some scrappy snacks during the long trek, but they had been spoiled by the good eating of the previous weeks.

For a hundred yards on every side, light shone out like the spokes of a wheel. Its rim was violet shadow and then darkness. Nothing moved. The scene was duplicated on the scanner, which had been switched to operate on a bank of energy cells. Anders gave the stand down and everyone climbed out of space gear. Power section personnel, whose cabins were in the end trailer, doubled temporarily with communications and navigation.

Miranda's door was nearest the entry hatch and as Munro came through unclipping his helmet, she met him with a tall glass of pale green liquid, cold enough to frost the outside.

'Pianist's reward. Come in and listen to your recital.'

He fought a half-hearted rearguard action. 'We're needed up in control.'

'Leave your suit here and we'll come back.'

Even with the acceleration couches swung clear, it was a tight fit to get fourteen into the control centre. Dag Fletcher found himself very much aware of Karen who was his neighbour at the chart spread. She had not changed completely out of space kit. She was wearing a moulded inner suit which fitted from wrists to ankles like a thin sheath. Square cut at the neck, the pale turquoise ribbed plastic underlined every curve. Auburn hair and golden brown skin.

Anders put in the log entry. 'Day 36.' He looked at his watch. 'Correction. Day 37, 0030 hours. Halted in darkness. Latitude as charted.' He went on to give the routine summary of scheduled information for the record.

'Anything to report, Karen?'

'No forward plan. I'll make a survey at first light. I believe we shall be within a day's journey of the sea. Possibly within sight. As a matter of interest for the log, there might be a picture of one of the hill-billies on this capsule.'

She passed up the microfilm to Myers who was standing behind the chart table and able to reach the scanner remote feed.

Under magnification, what they had deduced was clearly true. The camouflage broke down and revealed discreet identities. Small figures were crouched under concealing cloaks; there was a greater impression of movement though, than had been apparent to the naked eye. Then there was one sequence that made it worth while. Caught in the act of slinging a shot, one of the creatures rose to a kneeling position, brought an arm round in a circular swinging movement and let go with a round pebble in a thonged sling. Then he dropped down again. Myers reeled back for the optimum picture and held it steady. Then he began to blow it up until it filled the scanner.

It was a hominid. Short and broad with powerful shoulders and barrel chest. Very muscular thighs and upper arms tapering to relatively fine feet and hands. Lightly furred, with a silver grey fuzz. A shock of darker grey hair. Recognisably human features in general organisation; but every detail unexpected. Broad, almost circular face, more concave than convex. Like the round, shallow dish face of an owl, but without the predatory beak. A short snout with wide nostrils. Eyes round and unblinking separated by two eye widths. Round mouth, rimmed by rubbery lips, like a section of black hose turned back on itself. The ears gave the clue to their behaviour. Very delicate looking, set on either side of the spherical head like grey membranous trumpets.

Miranda said: 'He's got daffodil ears.'

Karen said, 'No wonder Dan took them by storm. Probably ears have developed sensitivity to recompense for very quiet voices. After all you have to match your receiver to your transmitter.'

Fletcher said, 'More likely they interfered with a signal they were all receiving. It upset their co-ordination.'

'It's as well we didn't have the picture before we went through the pass. Everyone might have been keen on a long detour.'

Anders went on to close the meeting—'No more tonight. We'll have a look ahead in the morning and see what lies between here and the sea. Can you organise some coffee and sandwiches, Susan?'

'Ready and waiting.'

'Until tomorrow then.'

The pool of light remained untroubled. Dag Fletcher took first watch and, as he handed over to Alvirez, he said, 'Nothing stirring. Just switch Dan over to replay every now and then.'

'Check.'

As the light strengthened, Bennett, doing the final spell of duty, could see where they had arrived. They were farther out from the hills than he had expected. The line of low peaks was some miles back. Immediately in front, the stony scrub stretched away with a very gradual fall and then appeared to flatten. The lie of the ground was concealed by the beginnings of vegetation. A change in the soil or the presence of water and with the prevailing high temperature, there would be everything to favour growth. From modest beginnings there was a build-up to full-scale jungle farther on.

Fletcher came in, wearing a space-suit with the helmet tipped back. 'At the risk of exacerbating the sex war, I'll go up and take a look. Give me a hand with the reel. You'll need a suit to use the intercom.'

'I'll pick it up on the way out.'

As they dropped through the entry port, faint sounds of basic Turkish Delight music filtered from Miranda's cabin. Outside the amplified Highland Games medley was going out at full strength.

'Our indefatigable music lover is having a field day,' said Bennett. 'It's not often an artist gets such immediate recognition.'

'Switch him off the public transmission anyway. He'll be getting a split personality.'

At two hundred feet, Dag signalled for a halt. There was no need to go any further. They were within sixty miles of the coast. In the growing, cinnamon-tinted light, the distant sea was a shining band on the horizon. Intervening, a belt of thick forest land. Unlike the more northerly forest of their first landing; there was a richness of foliage and a depth of undergrowth that looked ominous. He ranged to left and right with the binoculars. Tongues of the barren scrub ran into the forest and from the shore some inlets and grey-white strips of sand led back. By careful choice, it might be possible to cut down the width of forest to be crossed to about twenty miles. But that would be enough to make a major barrier. Two or three miles a day would be good going, if they had to fell and clear every foot of the way. Well, Karen could report on that. The advance view would give him an hour or two to think about it. He called down to Bennett, 'O.K. take it in,' and the balloon came down like an elevator.

He was back in the control room talking about the next stage to Anders, when the hard working balloon took off with its usual observer. Dag wondered momentarily whether Karen had seen him go up or not. Then he reflected that she would, no doubt, go up in any case. Not an easy one to deflect from a set purpose.

'We can go down one of the inlets into the jungle and then work on a bearing to the nearest sand bar. It will be slow but sure enough. We could range for days on either side and still have to come to it in the end.'

'I agree,' said Anders. 'There might be a quicker way than felling, though. What about demolition with small rocket charges?'

'The tangle might take as long to clear up as systematic felling. But it's worth a try.'

'It's a pity we're short of fuel, the rockets could clear a path.'

'Chad might have some ideas.'

Dag moved over to the window and found that Karen was just outside his range of vision. The taut line cut across the top of the port. He followed it down. Smith was standing with one hand on the power feed to the reel. There was a very slight air flow from the sea and the balloon was changing direction. Smith was looking up and following it. Then he appeared to make some adjustment to the winch. The balloon gained height rapidly. The end of the line whipped free. Smith made no move.

He was still standing there when Dag reached him. Then he seemed to snap out of some private reverie.

He said, 'The cable came free.'

'Not without help. I've already used it once today. It was all right then.'

Smith appeared to be genuinely confused.

'I didn't touch it.'

'I saw you make an adjustment. However, this is not the time to go into it.'

At about five hundred and fifty feet, still rising and gently drifting back towards the hills, Karen was clearly working to release the valve and bring the balloon down.

'She won't get it down within ten miles of here,' said Dag. He went back at a run to Anders.

'Pete, Karen's broken free in the balloon and she's drifting back into the hills. I'll get out after her in the power suit. Run this film in the scanner and you'll get a compass bearing on the best breakthrough. I suggest you make a start. We'll be back as soon as we can.'

'Right.'

Within minutes, the power suit was picking its zombie way back up the slope.

CHAPTER FOUR

'HOLD it there.'

Anders climbed down from the lead truck and walked ahead to the end of the tongue of bare scrub. An unbroken wall of multi-coloured vegetation faced them and hemmed them in on two sides. Fletcher had been gone two hours and they had moved slowly down the finger of desert. He was joined by John Alvirez and then Fergusson.

'We'll camp here and work ahead for a mile or so and then move.'

Smith left the driving seat and strolled back to the power section. He spoke to Lew Randle.

'That lot's going to take some shifting.'

'That's for sure.'

'I don't fancy being stuck here. There could be a place though.'

'Meaning?'

'Nothing yet. But if Fletcher gets himself knocked off on his balloon hunt, there might be less enthusiasm for all this covered wagon stuff. We could find somewhere comfortable and wait for a ship. There's bound to be one hitting Pelorus eventually. Set up a robot signal and relax.'

'Does anybody else think like that?'

'Craig and Myers might be persuaded.'

'Work on it then.'

'Check.'

The opportunity to sound out Craig came an hour later.

Anders stood with Chad Fergusson on the trunk of a felled tree and looked along the twisted tangle of debris caused by its fall. The whole crew had put in an hour's hard labour to sort out some viable technique for clearing a path. Methods of felling and dragging, used before, were no good here. There, the trees had been individual giants with little undergrowth; spaced, so that selective cutting produced a wide avenue. Here, the trees were close set and the small spaces between them were filled, chest high, with a tangle of minor growth. Sometimes a tree, although cut through, would refuse to fall and had to be dragged down by the overworked half track.

The only sure way was to clear back, a bit at a time, from the entry point. At the end of the hour, they had penetrated forty feet on a narrow front. In a ten hour day—and it would be slavery—they might make one tenth of a mile. Twenty miles in two hundred days.

Smith cut power to the vibrator and spoke to Andy Craig.

'You might as well try emptying a lake with a teaspoon. We'll be falling over long grey beards before we get through this lot.'

'Think of all the back pay you'll get.'

'That you might get.'

'What do you mean?'

'Alec won't draw it for one. Neither will anybody else if we go on dragging this beat-up bastard of a rocket around. If we'd set up a proper camp in the first place and used the ship for power, Alec would still be on the right side of the line.'

'Could be.'

'You're damn right it could be. Anyway this looks like the end of the way. Next chance, I, for one, vote for staying put. What about you?'

'I'll think about it.'

Smith slung the vibrator kit over a burly shoulder and picked his way back into the open. Medium height, very broad shoulders, barrel chest, he had short, jet black hair which came to an aggressive peak in the centre of his forehead. A first class engineer; ratings in this direction were so high that they outweighed lower ratings on some other sociometrics on his space ticket. He was inclined to be a barrack room lawyer on all issues of service pay and conditions. It definitely rankled with him that the No. 1 and No. 2 of any ship were always navigators.

Craig, fair, angular, slow speaking, was in the long tradition of Scottish engineers. Inclined to be stubborn and argumentative, the only scheme he could be enthusiastic about would be one he had thought of himself. He was too cautious in temperament to commit himself quickly to anything.

The whole party gathered in the centre of the laager, where Miranda, whose costume became more basic with every degree south, and Susan, who seemed untouched by changes of climate, had set up the cooking pots. Wood smoke was drifting back towards the hills and fresh meat was cooking on spikes. 1430 hours. Twenty-nine degrees Centigrade. Hot for forestry. They had been working stripped to the waist; but humidity was higher here and it was not comfortable. There was no conversation as each one helped himself to food and began to eat. Everyone felt that a critical point in the journey had been reached.

Ven Smith parked himself next to Ralph Myers in the shade of the leading module. Myers was on the strength of the communications section; but doubled as biologist and ship's doctor. Indeterminate in colouring, above medium height, heavy, unsmiling cast of features, he was not an easy man to get to know. He had been on *Interstellar Two-Five* for five voyages and had resented some of the new-broom tactics of the First Officer. When Smith opened the conversation, he was watching Miranda with expressionless eyes. It was no chore. She was visually the most interesting thing in sight. He went on doing it.

'Chances of getting through this lot don't look too good.'

'No.'

'There's something to be said for finding a site and waiting to be picked up. Bound to be missed in a month or two. Inter-Galactic Rescue Service will be doing a search. I expect you'd like to have a look round for biology gen?'

'Yes.'

'If this goes on, we could press for a crew conference and get a new decision. It takes five. Craig and Lew Randle are thinking that way.'

Myers took his eyes off Miranda. A tribute to Smith's perseverance, since at that moment she was bending over the fire towards him.

'So who would be number five, if I came in with you?'

'One of the girls probably. Miranda doesn't mind much where she is. Nor does Susan there. Or possibly Bennett. He's getting fed up.'

'All right. We'll have to see how it goes then.'

Myers walked across to the fire to get another skewer of barbecued meat and Smith went off, reasonably satisfied that he was making progress.

The balloon hunter himself was well back in the hills and pacing now below the free swinging end of its mooring rope. Karen had succeeded in regulating the valve, so that the balloon was losing height. As Fletcher was baulked by a terrace wall, the rope touched down for the first time and its drag slowed the drift.

Close packed stones made a smooth twelve foot wall in front of him. Reaching up, he was still over two feet short of a hold on top. Extensor capability was built in the left arm. He slipped his hand out of the gauntlet and worked the con-

C

trol on the external chest console with his right. He reflected that it would be a very quick way of losing an arm, if the relay struck and the mechanism operated before the inner gauntlet grip were released. The arm lengthened to the ledge and he turned the hand until the fingers lipped over. Then he retracted and the suit rose up the wall until he was able to grip with the other hand. At an increasing speed, the half ton of refined power pack lifted itself up and over.

As the stub visio eye on the dome levelled with the top, he saw the rope thirty yards away. At the same time a familiar muffled hammer blow on the forehead announced that he had company.

It was a closely run thing. The cumbersome suit was not built for speed. Sinking almost a foot in soft earth at every step, he pounded along to grab the rope; only a few yards ahead of the nearest competitor. He had time to notice that the end was complete with its spring toggle that snapped it on to the next section. Then he looped it into a spare ring on his belt and began to fend off the circle of hominids that came crowding in.

Karen had watched the action and was making no further attempt to lose height. He looked up at the slim silver figure two hundred and fifty feet above him. The intercom on the power suit could act as a local exchange. He called her up.

'Stay up there if you can. I'll tow you along.'

'Thank you very much. I'd advise movement as of now. There must be a thousand or more of these hominids on the way. They're coming over from the next valley.'

Instead of answering, he began to move. The drag of the balloon was hardly noticed by the massive suit. The press of men was unimportant. He shook two off each arm and went forward at a slow walk. A group formed in front and refused to move as he bore down on them.

Something about their eyes bothered him. He realised that they were afraid, but were in some way forced to the action

they were taking. As before Dan Munro's music had interfered with their co-ordination, they were acting together. It
was as though one mind directed all the bodies. But not at
once. As if the mind were at a distance and had to sort out
data and then transmit fresh instructions.

Karen's voice came through the small speaker in the dome.
'I believe that is so. The ones over the hill are acting together.
There doesn't seem to be a leader. They look as though they're
all tuned in to some communal signal.'

He realised that she was answering his unspoken thoughts.
'You're not doing too badly yourself.'

'Why do you say that?'

'You've just read pretty accurately what was in my mind.'

'Oh.'

Fletcher ploughed through the group and put up the speed.
He reached the edge of the terrace and began to run along
the top of the wall. It was easier going and for a time it was
in the direction he wanted to go. There semed to be a lull
on.

Karen said, 'They've turned their attention to the balloon.
How tough is it?'

Stones were thudding into the fabric above her head. A
sudden sharp intake of breath and he knew she had been hit.
The space-suit was not designed to stand short range sling
shots.

They reached the point where the wall curved away from
their direct route and he jumped down without checking his
stride. The heavy robot sank knee deep in the peaty soil and
he was stopped for a moment, then he was pressing on, along
harder ground, in the path used earlier by their convoy.

Karen said, 'We've got an even chance of getting through
this section before the lot from over the hill can turn into it.'

This seemed to be known to the hominids who were following them. They kept up a constant fire of sling shots at the
two targets. Fletcher was moving at maximum speed. Without

weapons, he could only rely on the overwhelming power of the suit to drive him through. Its materials were proof against most hazards, but a lucky shot on the chest console could do damage. Karen was more vulnerable.

She was saying, 'It's dawned on them that we might make it. They're all running. Looks like a river in flood.'

They were still thirty yards from the key junction when the leaders of the main force ran out and closed the path.

Fletcher began to wonder whether the suit would do it. Possibly it could trample its way through. It could hardly keep the line though. That was sure to be torn free.

Karen said, 'Don't worry about me. You've got to get back. I have an oblivion pill.' Her voice was steady and quiet.

The possibility that she might go out in this way was suddenly vivid. He knew that she was very special to him as a human being.

He said, 'There's no question of that, Karen. We're going back, both. Hang on to your hat.'

Then he was taking the right hand wall of the pass in giant steps. Working the extensor arm with meticulous accuracy, he had risen two terrace heights before the crowd below had crossed the first patch of ground. Then he was thudding along a wall rim.

More and more hominids had crowded out on to the pass, until it was choked from side to side; but he was beyond their point of entry and began to drop down again. On the hard ground, he coaxed every ounce of speed out of the pounding piston legs. The balloon was being forced down by the angle of drag until Karen was barely a hundred feet above the heads of the following mass. Stones were regularly hitting her now and drummed a constant tattoo on the broad back of the robot.

When the stones stopped, he was a few seconds sorting out what had happened.

Karen said, 'It's as if there were an invisible barrier across the pass and the hills. They're lined up along it. I think we're going to be all right.'

He slowed down and spun the prismatic eye to look backwards. From ground level the effect was probably more dramatic than the bird's eye view. From edge to edge, out of sight both ways, the road back was a continuous line of grey hominids. Motionless, staring. They were still there when he turned again to look back at the curve of the pass which would take him out of sight.

The balloon had gained height as he slowed down. Now it dipped again as he picked up speed. There was no point in hauling in. Karen might as well ride. They passed the area of the last camp with the ashes of the fire still warm.

The power suit with its balloon had been visible for some time from the laager and Alvirez walked back to meet them. Fletcher switched on the outside receiver which put the conversation on the net for the aerialist.

'Glad to see you back, Dag. And, of course, Ginger, up there. I expect she's just playing "hard to get". But this is carrying it too far. Snags have come up. We could be a year getting through this strip.'

'Well, we have a year.'

'Explain that to Smith and one or two others. My spies tell me they have a "colonise Pelorus" group.'

'What's the problem?'

'Undergrowth. Close set trees. We'd be lucky to do a mile a week.'

'Thanks for the warning. I'll think about it. First of all we need some food.'

They reached the winch and Alvirez took the cable and fixed it to the free clip. There was no obvious explanation of how it had ever become detached. As it came in, Fletcher began to dig himself out of the power suit. When Karen touched down, he was able to catch her as she crumpled forward.

He carried her along the narrow corridor of the command module and to her cabin, which was next to the Captain's. Sliding back the door, he manœuvred her in feet first and then propped her against the wall whilst he swung down the acceleration couch which doubled for a bed. When he turned round, she had hinged back the silver visor and was tugging warily at the seals.

'If there's any muscle without a bruise, I don't know where it is.'

'Relax then. I'll help you.'

He eased out the seals in a wide oval round her shoulders, then shot back the clips and lifted off the entire casque. Her face had a pallor under the tan and there were lines of strain round her eyes; but she made no complaint when he had to move her to get at the line of seals and clips down the left side of the suit. Then he peeled it away and she was standing against the wall looking more than ever like a sketch for the Age d'Or. Instead of the quilted inner suit, she was wearing rudimentary shorts and a thin shirt of fine semi-transparent white linen.

When he lifted her over to the bed she bit her lip against the pain.

'I'll get Susan to come in and look at you. You need a massage with some of that muscle cream.'

He had time to notice the cabin and register that she had given it the impress of her personality. Pale pastel-shaded walls added space to its dimensions. A small abstract, ovals and spirals predominantly in greens subtly changing to blues and greys.

She looked younger and very vulnerable. She said, 'Thank you,' quietly.

'It isn't necessary. Left hands don't thank right hands.' As he said it, he knew that it was true and that there was a growing unity between them. Steps along the corridor sounded like Susan's, coming to see if she could help. He bent over and kissed her forehead. A sort of sighting shot in their new relationship.

'See you later.'

Then he was outside and saying to Susan, 'You'll be welcome. Karen's been providing target practice. As the target.'

Outside, he sought out Chad Fergusson.

'What's it like Chad?'

'Not good.'

'No bright ideas?'

'We're short of power. Given the tools we'd be through to-day. As it is, this could be impossible.'

'Burning?'

'Might help; but the real chore is clearing up the rubble to make a usable lane for heavy, wheeled traffic.'

'Heavy, wheeled traffic?'

'Yes. You know, these.' He tapped the nearest one.

'Suppose they were not so heavy?'

'Any gain that way would give a bigger power margin for dragging through the debris.'

'Playing balloon man has given me a thought. What's the lift on these balloons?'

'Could be a ton or so on the small ones with maximum inflation. Quite considerable on the big one.'

'Suppose we moved the cradles one at a time, with the three balloons giving optimum lift. Perhaps we could force through, without much clearing up on the ground?'

'You're in the wrong section. It might just work. I'm inclined to think we'd be better without wheels in that case. Skid along like a sledge over the tangle. Crushed vegetation would be a lubricant. Lighten each one in turn, then ferry the stuff along under the balloons. Not bad at all. We're in business.'

'One thing though. How does the half-track get on?'

'It doesn't. The power suit can pull, if we get the friction sorted out. Frail human flesh will have to take a hand and walk alongside with levers to fend off and ease the burden over awkward lifts. By the way, Ven Smith is going to love this. He's drumming up support for a sit down. I'm sorry to say that he's got Craig and Randle interested. Must be something about engineering that encourages mutiny.'

'I'll fix Smith.' Fletcher had only postponed the showdown in that direction. He wanted to know precisely how the balloon link had come unclipped. He went on, 'Get the other balloons out. Harness up to the cone section. Trial run in half an hour.'

Chad went off to get things moving. Dag Fletcher turned away and found that Karen was behind him.

'How long have you been there?'

'Long enough to appreciate that Spencer was right. You really are an asset.'

Paul V. Spencer, the Space Corporation Chairman, was about as tactful as a rhinoceros. He must have been giving Dag an advance billing, calculated to sour labour relations from the start.

'Praise indeed.'

'Susan says there's a move to make a permanent camp. If you hadn't come up with a scheme, it would have been hard to argue against.'

'We don't know yet whether it will work. But one way or another we're going on. There's nothing on Pelorus to interest me. Except you, of course.'

'That was an after-thought.'

'Yes, after looking at you. This light does something to your hair.'

The cinnamon light of Pelorus gave her hair an intensity of colour which was almost startling. She was looking at him in silence. He went on, 'Anyway you'll be leaving at the same time.'

'When?'

'No firm booking given. How are the bruises?'

'Bruise. One. Continuous. Not too bad if I don't bend.'

They crossed to the fire and helped themselves to skewers of meat.

Chad Fergusson was not one to hang about when there was clear action to take. He called Craig.

'Andy. I want you to rig some kind of yoke and towing harness on the power suit. Something that won't break, no matter what. O.K.?'

'Check.'

Then he called Smith and Randle. 'Break out the rest of the weather balloon stock. Including Big Bertha. I want lifting harness arranged on the cone section cradle for a start. Biggest lift at the bows. The idea is to lighten the load and tow it over the rough path. Can do?'

'Whose idea was that?' Smith asked the question in a tone which showed what he thought of it.

Fergusson looked at him reflectively for a long pause.

'Get moving, Ven. Yours but to do and die. It could be the latter, the way you're going on.'

The rest of the crew were coming out to make a start and Chad explained the new tactic. Alvirez and Bennett went ahead with the biggest vibrator and began cutting out selected trees. Munro in the power suit pushed them over. Myers and Robertshaw trimmed off the larger projections with hand vibrators. By the end of the afternoon they had a rough gulley just over a mile deep into the jungle.

When they crawled back into the camp, Anders, Fletcher and the three engineers had fixed the leading section ready for towing. Beside it were a dozen trimmed saplings to use as levers. A mesh of cordage led up to the three straining balloons. It was beginning to look feasible.

After an hour's break, some of the heat was going out of the day. Chad elected to do the first session with the power

c*

suit. He wanted to feel for himself the mechanical balance of the arrangement.

The clumsy cradle towed forward easily. Three men with levers on each side lifted its bows to take the first obstacle and it rocked and swayed forward. The levers became props as it took a sheer and bore down on its side. Then it levelled out over a mass of springy undergrowth and foliage.

Chad clambered along, sometimes waist deep. The robot suit was not developing anything like its full power.

For the attendant pole men it was a mad scramble. No one had come out in a space suit and without the intercom Fergusson was incommunicado.

Dag forced his way ahead and placed himself where he must be seen by the suit's scanning eye. He held up both hands in a universal mime gesture for stop and waited to be trampled into the ground. Chad came to a reluctant halt and began to break out the helmet seals. Finally he lifted it off.

'What in the name of hell is it now? We're doing fine. It goes like a bomb.'

'Only for you. For the infantry, it goes as if it wasn't on our side. It's going to be an all hands job with the levers. Even then you'll have to slow it down a bit.'

Standing still for a breather, they became aware of the noises. There was a staccato hammering, which filled in all the gaps left by other intermittent sounds. Deep coughing barks at uneven intervals echoed by another of higher pitch. Howls with a dying fall like a coyote. A mush of un-identifiable minor clatter. The atmosphere was thickly oppressive.

They left the module and trekked back the hundred yards to the main camp.

Alvirez had a long gash from shoulder to elbow where a falling branch had scored through shirt and skin. Miranda brought out a first aid kit and began to dress it.

'Thank you, Miranda,' he said, 'you are as useful as you are beautiful.'

It had been a long day. She was too tired to say anything.

This was the first time that the sections of the ship had been widely separated and although the balloons were visible over the trees, there was a feeling that the cone section was very vulnerable. No one was comfortable about it. Anders said to Fletcher privately, 'What about the cone, Dag? We couldn't do any good from here if it were attacked.'

'Let's face it, we couldn't do much good *here* if we were attacked. But I see what you mean. Before the light goes, I'll send a couple of men down. They can seal up and spend the night there. Suit intercom'll give contact over that distance.'

'Do that. Anything else?'

'One thing. I'd like to look through the crew confidential files. I did have a quick flip over them, when I came on board; but I'd like a closer look.'

'Help yourself.' Anders fished out a small flat key. He and Fletcher were the only two to have access to the crew records. It was a reasonable angle that the First Officer should want to find out as much as possible.

On the way to the Captain's cabin, Fletcher stopped to pass the good news of extra duty down the pipeline.

'Chad. Get hold of Lew Randle and Dan Munro will you. I want them both ready to go along to the cone and look after it tonight. They can do four-hour stints, watch about. Seal the hatches. Take suits for the intercom. Report every fifteen minutes to the duty man here.'

'Check.'

Outside, the sky shaded down into intense violet black. Lights came up on the modules and made themselves a clear space in the gloom. Down the track, a subdued glow showed that Munro and Randle were in position. Dag worked on, listening patiently to the lengthy records spoken by the quiet dispassionate voice of a security official.

Eavesdropping on Karen's tape was almost like taking unfair advantage. But there was nothing there which he could not have dictated himself. Excellent course ratings. Security rating. A plus for background. School and college records, exemplary. Extra diploma in Art. That was an unusual touch. Ratings on all physical and temperamental traits in the top bracket. Pain tolerance high. That was true enough. He left it at that. If Karen had any faults, he didn't want to know.

Miranda Dolon had a good press. There was nothing there which could prove subversive. Some wag in security had pencilled *Amor Vincit Insomnia* on the small ivorine tablet below her name.

Having given himself a standard, he played Ven Smith's tape. He was immediately struck by a dubitative quality. It was conceded that he was top line in his profession; but there was something conveyed in the voice of the recorder that sowed doubt. He played it all through again. Then he found it. One rating was out of line. In one sphere alone, a high rating was not good. Suggestibility was several points too high for normal acceptance in deep space personnel. Only the very strong ratings elsewhere had pulled him through.

Dag went on. He paid special attention to that rating in other cases. It might be useful to know who could be most relied on to keep facts firmly in line. Not unexpectedly, Len Robertshaw had the lowest rating he had ever seen. He was the best bet for a detached view. Anders' was low, so was his own, Fergusson and Alvirez were next. Miranda surprised him by being almost as low on the rating as Robertshaw. A very level-headed girl, then. Others were about average with Myers, Craig and Randle nearest to the danger mark.

When he had finished, he went back into the control cabin. Pete Anders had taken first watch and Dag was next on duty. He handed over the key.

'Thanks, Pete. There is something. All these characters—particularly Smith—who are binding about the journey, have a doubtful rating on suggestibility. It may be coincidence. There may be nothing in it. On the other hand it could make difficulties if things get really tough. They're a potential fifth-column in certain circumstances.'

Anders had been long enough in space to know what was implied there. On some planets mind warfare was advanced and only the most rigidly stable crew men could survive it.

'It's as well we know that. But it doesn't alter anything. We have to go on.'

'I agree.'

'I'll turn in. Everything's quiet. As far as I know, everyone's had enough for today.'

'Right.'

Hatches on the modules had been sealed. The scanner showed the tongue of scrub and the gash in the jungle ahead with a dim halo of light above the concealed cone section. He sat in his own chair at the control console, tapping the desk with an ivorine check tablet.

There was a slight movement at the hatch. Without giving any indication that he heard, he casually skimmed the white strip into its slot and began to stand up. Simultaneously, he slid back the recessed lid of the locker, which lay below the chart spread. As he turned, he took out the small Laser pistol that lay there. In a smooth continuity of movement, he completed the enchainment by bringing up the narrow muzzle to bear precisely on the centre of Karen's medallion as she came forward.

She said, 'Friend. I think.'

'Excuse this. I'm jumping at shadows.'

'It could be necessary.'

She moved stiffly forward and sat with great care on the acceleration couch. Then she slowly manœuvred one leg at a time until she was sitting forward with arms locked round her knees. An elastic bell of silky, auburn hair swung forward and hid her face.

'How are the honourable wounds?' He put away the pistol and slid back the covering square.

'Stiff and sore.' Her voice was almost inaudible. Dag leaned over and, with a hand on each shoulder, rolled her back on to the soft couch. She stayed in a compact ball, still holding her knees. He sat beside her and bent down, until they were looking into each other's eyes at point blank range. Suddenly, she straightened out, and, as he kissed her lips, her arms went round his neck pulling his mouth to hers. Her lips were full and soft and slightly tremulous.

The miniature screens on the secondary consoles had been left in circuit, so that the duty officer faced a copy of the main scanner picture wherever he looked. Ahead of him on the power desk, the small screen blinked. Even as he saw a faint flush of colour beneath the golden brown tan on Karen's cheeks and felt the quicker rhythm of her breathing, there was an alarm signal sounding in the computer depths of his mind. Then he knew why. The lights on the distant module had gone out.

She said, 'Perhaps they've turned them out.'

Without asking her, he knew that she had not seen the picture. There was some kind of direct transfer between them.

The moment of indecision, before he spoke, was interpreted as if they had one mind.

She went on, 'Don't worry about me, Dag. I know you have to go and find out.'

He said seriously, 'Karen, even apart from this mental thing there's something ahead for us. There's never been anyone I felt like this about. We'll take it slowly. Don't doubt it. Whatever happens, we'll make out.'

For some seconds they looked closely into each other's eyes.

Each felt that it was in some way like looking through a succession of mirrors and meeting oneself again from a new angle.

Then Dag said gently, 'It has to be now,' and pressed the alarm.

Urgent bleeps began to sound through the module. Karen moved cautiously to her own 'blast off' station under the periscope mounting and lowered the acceleration cradle. Dag began to call up Randle and Munro.

Anders was first to join them.

'What's going on, Dag?'

'Something's happened at the cone. No lights. No signal.'

'They're on a schedule for calling up on the quarter. They might not be near a suit. It's a low amplification job.'

'I hope you're right. The quarter's coming up now.'

Fletcher repeated the urgent signals which would send any trained spaceman to a transmitter by simple reflex action. The rest of the key personnel of the control cabin had filtered in and were in position at their 'blast off' stations. Dag put the signal on to a robot sender and cut the local repeat.

He said, 'I'll get the power suit out and take a look down there.'

Anders nodded agreement.

'Look after yourself.'

Five minutes later, Dag was standing by the main exit hatch where Miranda, correctly dressed in her all white space-suit was waiting to work the lock.

Remembering his recent researches into crew statistics, he said, 'Give me your direct communication link.'

Duly plugged in, they could speak without being overheard on the net. 'Keep an eye on Smith for me. Not alone. You can mention this to John Alvirez. Try to ensure that at least two people are always with him.'

'Anything to oblige a superior officer.'

But he knew it would be carried out to the letter.

Built-in light units sent a powerful beam down the ragged gulf. He ploughed through the tangle of branches as if they were grass stalks. The bluff stern of the cradle appeared in front of him. Intact. He climbed the side and began to search. There was no trace that any man or animal had been on board. He turned his attention to the great silver cone. The twin hatches in the base, normally internal corridor seals, were closed. He spun the release wheels which operated from either side.

Munro was lying just inside. He had been trying to get out. His neck was broken as Alec Ross's had been. Fletcher had to stoop to walk along the low corridor in this section. Most of the space was filled with hydroponic tanks and some of the liquid gas containers. A pulsing red light in the power suit dome told him that the air was unfit to breathe.

Lew Randle was lying over the cylinder which had poisoned him. He had turned it on himself.

CHAPTER FIVE

IF it had only to be done once, it would have been not too bad. Twice, even would have been endurable. It was the third run that broke everybody's heart.

Dag Fletcher insisted that the three modules should be moved up together at the end of each day's run. In the morning, the whole party worked to open up a rough canyon; biting another two miles into the thick, steam-heated jungle. Then, three back-breaking trips brought up the cradles. The trolley stayed back with the last mover, to winch back the balloons on a long thin trailing line.

The first journey showed up the snags. Then the heavy centre section found a few more that no one had thought of. Coming at the end, the power module made every awkward move in the book.

Once they were together, Fletcher drove everyone on to clear a circle for the evening camp. It was not much protection; but it gave them some elbow room and the lights made a moat of brilliance which had to be crossed.

At the end of the sixth day, when the robot suit stopped pulling and the power module was in place, they stood still where they were, stupid with fatigue.

Dag had been working next to Karen on the lever detail. She was out on her feet. Patches of sweat darkened her yellow one-piece work suit. Damp hair stuck to her cheeks. Her eyes looked enormous. He put an arm round her shoulders. Before she could protest, he picked her up and began to carry her towards the centre module. In spite of herself, she relaxed momentarily and closed her eyes. He felt the slackening of her body and kissed her neck lightly. The velvet smooth skin tasted slightly salt. Then she had struggled free and was walking beside him.

'You must be just as tired as I am.'

'I have the advantage of having you to look at.'

'That's a pretty speech for the end of the day.'

He helped her through the hatch and went back to the final chore of cutting out a circle of trees for the clearing.

Susan Yardley had been inside for the last half hour. When Chad finally dug himself out of the power suit and the whole party reassembled inside, a fresh coffee smell was wreathing out from the navigator's wardroom. The crowd spilled over into the narrow corridor and Alvirez sat on the floor next to Miranda. Slowly, the honey blonde head tilted sideways. She was asleep when it came to rest on his shoulder. He swivelled her round until her head was in his lap. Deep regular breathing was undisturbed. Then he went on eating. Sure that every situation has an advantage in it somewhere, he lodged his coffee cup on the flat buckle of the wide bronze belt, which she wore over a black one-piece work suit. It rose and fell in slow rhythm.

'That's exploitation if you like,' said Myers.

When the meal finished, darkness was complete and the lights were blazing. Dag cornered Chad Fergusson and Anders.

'Two things; we can't go on much longer without some protection against the heat. I suggest we work in space-suits tomorrow. It might slow us down, but there'll be less fatigue. Secondly, we are virtually unarmed. Can you, Chad, work out any kind of weapon from the supplies we have? One thing did cross my mind. Some kind of flame-thrower, using what's left of the combustion chamber lining. Rocket fuel capsules from the spare suits. I can't visualise the details.'

'You've said more than enough.' Chad Fergusson was looking resigned. 'It could be done. But for when? I'm bushed right now.'

Anders said, 'We've got away with it so far. But any determined physical attack would finish us. I don't believe, though, that we've had the last of the mental infiltration. There's no doubt in my mind that Randle was influenced to attack Munro and then forced to open the cylinder. And don't forget that Alec was killed in the same way. But there's one thing that stands in our favour on the second affair.'

Chad said, 'I can't wait to hear what that was. To my simple mind there was nothing good about it.'

'The lights. There was no advantage to be gained by having the lights put out. To the contrary in fact. It warned us that something was wrong. Therefore, I believe Randle was not completely controlled and deliberately put them out, knowing someone would take a look.'

Fletcher said, 'That could be true. Except in the one particular, Lew Randle was a first-class crew man. But on the other matter, I'd be glad to have that armament as soon as you can get round to it.'

'O.K. You win. Give me ten minutes and I'll make a start. You and Pete can give me a hand. John Alvirez too, if Miranda can spare him.'

When the meal finished, the four men made their way back into the power module where Chad had improvised a work room.

Before going out, Alvirez carried Miranda to her room. She was still asleep when he laid her on the narrow acceleration couch which doubled as a bunk. He took off her sandals and unclasped her bronze belt. Brown feet with straight toes; slim strong ankles. Dust and blood from a deep scratch over the instep. In the toilet dispenser, he found some tissues and a plastic tube of water. Quickly he washed them. Even asleep she was more interesting than an engineering problem. Reluctantly, he went to the door. As he was going out, she said,

'Thank you, John.' But when he turned round, her eyes were closed and she was asleep again.

Two hours later a prototype flame-thrower was nearing completion. Chad had worked personally on the tube, giving it a breech and firing toggle to ignite rocket charges. The other three had produced a swivel mounting from acceleration couch gymbals. A gunner would be able to sit behind the tube and make a full circle turn in any plane. Strapped in, he could cover any conceivable angle of approach.

Dag said, 'This makes me feel more comfortable. One of these on each module will give us protection against any primitive attack.'

Anders said, 'Always provided the operators stay on our side.'

'That, of course. How long now, Chad? I don't propose making the other two tonight.'

The answer was not given. A tremor shook the cradle, so that it swayed on its uneasy bed of brushwood and tumbled trunks. Inside the power module, they were virtually blind. Only the screens in the command cabin were giving a picture of the clearing.

There, Bennett was on watch and was looking with complete incredulity at the largest, bat-like flying carpet, he had ever seen. An airborne sting ray, twenty feet across and looking too solid and meaty to fly at all. After its dive at the power module, it levelled off and climbed in a wheeling half circle to make another run. He pulled on the alarm and urgent bleeps began to sound through the section.

Miranda was first to join Bennett. She looked at the black manta without any enthusiasm as it renewed its attack on the rear cradle. A squat head was lowered beneath the leading edge of the massive wings. A three foot length of splintered log projected both sides of the open crocodile snout.

'What does it want that for? There's plenty of wood about. Where's John?'

'All the top brass are busy over there, making a flame-thrower. Not before time seemingly.'

Craig, Smith, Robertshaw, Myers, Karen and Susan Yardley were crowding in. They watched the screen. Nobody moved. An inertia seemed to hold them. Dag's voice over the intercom stirred Bennett into action. He answered. 'We're under attack from a flying manta. It seems to be aiming to break up your cradle.'

'Is it possible to get across to you?'

Bennett watched the slow unwieldy climb of the great beast.

'You'd have half a minute at least if it was timed right.'

'Give me the signal when I should move.'

A further shuddering jar shook the power module and Bennett's voice came through. 'Move now.'

Dag was out and climbing over the bows of the cradle. Only ten yards separated him from the stern of the centre section. Judging distances, he leaped from log to log. He was within reach of the grips leading up, when an unsupported trunk dipped away under his feet and threw him into the tangle of boughs and foliage which floored the clearing

The manta had reached the apex of its turn and visibly checked its dive. Vast wings back pedalled as it re-aligned its flight. Then it was sweeping down into the gap between the two cradles.

Karen made an effort of will and pulled herself away from the screen. She said, 'Miranda, help me to get into the power suit.' Sharpened by danger, the thought-transfer link with Dag was clear as crystal. As if she were there, she knew that he was sheltering under a thick network of branches. With his eyes, she saw the scaly neck and head thrusting down in the gaps. Miranda said, 'I'm more experienced with that monster. Let me go. There's no danger.'

Two minutes later, the watchers in the cabin saw the familiar black dome of the power suit lumber into the open space at the rear of the module. Karen was objective enough to realise that Miranda was quite right and the venture was more likely to be successful with someone used to operating the robot.

Miranda began to climb down the holds on the outside of the cradle. The manta was still digging about in the tangle of logs. It filled the space between the cradles with a living black carpet. At the bottom rung, she paused for a moment and estimated distances. Then she jumped for the centre.

The effect was spectacular. A wild explosion of power and ferocity tore through the clearing. Rearing back, with convulsively thrashing wings, it showed its underside shading from black to drab grey, with two short powerful legs jerking and stabbing downwards. A black band under its throat was an arm of the power suit. Miranda had dropped centrally between the wings and was pulling its head back with at least half of the suit's potential strength. No organic matter could stand up to it. The head tore off.

Before the creature's nervous system had finished flailing the headless body about the clearing, Dag was climbing into the module followed by the robot suit. Inside, he tapped the black dome and spoke into the external mike.

'Thank you, Miranda. Finish off a good job by going across to the power module and telling Pete all about it. They might need your support to get back.'

She did not ask him how he knew who was in the suit. An uncomplicated girl, she took facts as she found them and got on with it.

No other manta appeared. Miranda carried back the completed flame-thrower as if it were weightless. Dag met the procession at the hatch.

'What range do you expect, Chad?'

'This is my very first flame-thrower, so I'll make no claims. Could be fifty yards.'

'Set it up on top and run a trial.'

They mounted it on a flat platform formed by one of the radiation shields. When it fired, a thin searing jet of white hot gas blasted its way out of the clearing and carved itself a path through the packed trees.

'That's more like it,' said Dag. 'We can deal with anything we're likely to meet with that. We'll mount one on each trailer. How much fuel?'

'Quite a lot. That blast used half a standard rocket charge for the space-suit packs. We must have five hundred spares.'

'Right. Sleep then. One thing about the long day on Pelorus —it's followed by a long night. We still have an hour or two and we'll delay the start tomorrow.'

Pete Anders brought the dictated record up to date on the morning of day fifty. Less than two miles of jungle separated the modules from a tongue of pale sand which pushed back like a fjord into the blue green jungle. That would be a reasonable stint for the day. Reasonable as reason now reckoned, after the long chore. They had made better time than they had any right to expect. Not without wear and tear on the cradles and on themselves. Still, there would be a spell on the beach.

The crew were sour with tiredness. In spite of regular isometric drill and first class basic physique, they were not equipped for the grind of the last weeks. Dynamic tension exercises kept up muscle tone on the long stretches of reduced weight flight, but this was work for primitives used to manual labour.

He spoke into the recorder. 'Day 50. Within two miles of clear ground. Crew morale good in the circumstances. Modules now armed with flame-throwers. No further mental infiltration.'

From the control cabin port, he could see Fletcher and Alvirez carrying out the vibrator set for the last stint of tree felling. They were joined by Miranda in a dazzling white space-suit. Then Bennett and Craig in steel grey, Craig still limping from a twisted knee. The two leading figures, silver and bronze, had stopped and were stooping over the vibrator, apparently checking through a power lead. The other three came up and made a compact group. A movement nearer the ship caught his eye. Ven Smith, identifiable by the steel-grey suit with crew number 11 back and front, had come out and was watching the others. Something wooden about his movements made Anders think about his last sentence on the log.

Smith turned back and passed out of direct vision. Without precisely knowing why, Anders tuned the scanner to pick him up. He was climbing rungs to get on to the top of the capsule. Why at this time? What was up there anyway? As he gave himself the answer, Anders was at the console bringing all intercom sets on a single net for an overriding, emergency call. He said, 'One to group. Emergency. Scatter. Smith on flame-thrower. May be dangerous.' Then he was moving out at a run.

As he opened the hatch, Smith reached for the flame-thrower and the clearing emptied. Anders had not yet put on a suit and the conversation went on without him.

Fletcher said, 'Two to group. Keep out of sight. Nobody is to try to rush the module. Concentrate on Smith. Empty your mind of everything else. Just Smith. Think this action over and over again. He is to stand up. Leave the gun and climb down. No more. Just that. Over and over again. Now.'

Minutes ebbed slowly away. Smith sat and manœuvred the gun through several arcs. Then he was still. Even from a distance it was possible to see indecision in his behaviour. Twice, he put his hands to the tubular frame of the seat as though to heave himself out and then dropped back and returned to making sweeps of the clearing. Then he appeared to come to a decision. He stood up and moved slowly to the rungs leading down.

Fletcher and Alvirez were on either side of him as he reached the ground.

Dag said, 'Come on, Ven. Time to go to work. You take a turn with the felling. What do you think of the flame-thrower?'

'Flame-thrower?'

'You've just been up there, testing the traverse.'

'No. I've just come from inside. What is this? Are you trying to tell me I don't know what I'm doing.'

'Could be. I have to warn you. Watch your actions. No blame on you, but you might be a target for outside influence. You certainly were up there.'

'Well that's just too bad, isn't it?'

It occurred to Dag that Smith might well know of his weakness. Crew men had access to their own records before each trip; except for Commander's confidential reports.

'All right, Ven. You can take it whichever way you like. Understand this though. If your survival is balanced against the survival of Two-Five, it's the ship every time for me.'

They worked through the morning in silence. The routine was established like clockwork. An hour before the midday break, they made out into the open. A barren strip of hard white sand and shale, which projected into the jungle like a pointed tongue. The sea was still out of sight at ground level; but from here, they would be able to refit the wheels and make good time. The midday meal was more cheerful than for some days past. Everyone saw the ragged avenue to the open as an escape route.

In spite of the busy noise of wild life, no one had had any success in getting anything for the pot.

Susan said, 'We haven't got the right techniques for a food gathering economy. There should be ritual purification. Cave painting before you go out. Fertility stuff. Someone should crawl down a rocket tube and paint a bison.'

'We could do that, John,' said Miranda. 'You could use my lipstick.'

The cone section went through in the best run of the whole trip. Tackles slung on standing trees at the edge of the hard ground swayed it up and the wheels went on. Then Chad dragged it clear before the balloons were winched back for the centre section. It was like coming off an assembly line.

More normal snags developed as the heavy command module ploughed its way through the springy track. Enthusiasm was waning. They were impatient to be done with the whole clumsy business. But in the end it was towed clear and joined the lead vehicle in the bright cinnamon light.

It was left to the power pack to fight its own rearguard action. As usual the track had been badly mauled by the other two. The pace fell to half what it had been with the cone. A hundred yards from the end, it made its last play.

At that point transfer had to be made to the thick end of a massive trunk. Most of the party were in readiness with levers in place to help the bows to lift on to it. Fletcher and Myers at one side, Anders and Smith at the other remained to steady it on its course. Just before the lift, there was a dip on to the two logs of uneven thickness which caused a sway over to Anders and Smith. This time the lower trunk had been forced even lower by the passage of the centre section. The power module lurched and passed its point of no return.

Smith flung himself clear. Anders ran forward, wedged in the prop and hung on.

For a moment there was balance, as the heel of the three-inch diameter pole dug itself into the heavy soil and the tip lodged in an overlap of the clinker built hull. But even with the balloons giving their maximum lift there was too much weight on the shoring beam.

Racing from the other side, Fletcher rounded the bluff bows of the cradle in time to see the support arch itself like a bow.

He shouted, 'Leave it, Pete. Get back!' as it broke with a single sharp crack like the snap of a stockwhip.

Plunging faster, after the check, the cradle bore down with inescapable speed. Before anyone could move, it had fallen free. Anders was borne down into the brushwood by the tumble home side.

The module itself remained, remarkably, in its chocks. Fletcher and Alvirez rammed home struts in case it should work loose. The others were standing in silence, taken aback by the suddenness of the event. Dag said, 'Two poles would have held it. Certainly it would have given Pete a chance to get clear. Did you know what you were doing, Smith?'

'We both saw it coming. I thought he would have the sense to get from under.'

'Instead he had the sense and the guts to do the job he was here to do.'

'Meaning?'

Karen's voice broke in on the net. 'Mantas, Dag.' He had time to say, 'Find cover in the trees.' The sky darkened over the narrow gulley.

In the jungle there was no danger. The massive delta wings were finding it difficult enough to drop into the narrow cleft. But they were likely to destroy the cradle if they were left. It was difficult to know how many were working at it. Looking identical, one dropped down and tore out a piece of timber, then, as it cleared the tree tops, another one made its run in.

Fletcher waited until one had begun its ponderous lift. He had worked round into the nearest point to the precariously leaning module. In a count of seven seconds flat, he had climbed behind the gun and was swinging the barrel to sight on the incoming manta. His extra weight, at that angle, made the props creak in protest. The head was invisible, so he aimed at the centre of the wing. At less than sixty feet range, he yanked down the firing toggle.

A flare of intense white light flashed through the gloom

in a ragged line. Momentarily, the underside of the manta was spotlighted in every scaly detail. Then the flame struck home. The whole centre backbone disintegrated. There was a moment when the bare, honeycomb structure of thin white bone was clear. Then half a ton of debris dumped itself beside the cradle.

Dag reloaded and took the next one as it came spilling over the lip of the gulf like a black wave. It remained in tattered fragments amongst the branches. In the gap before the next candidate, he spoke to Alvirez. 'Get along to the command module, John. On the way back, they might have a crack at it. Take Len for the other gun. We'll be along as soon as we can make it.'

'Check.'

Then he was busy again.

It was twenty minutes before the mantas had had enough. Nine had been dropped and the narrow gulley looked like a macabre slaughterhouse in the cinnamon light. In the silence Dag made a group call.

'Everybody in here. Craig and Smith with supports. Chad can lift the cradle back with the power suit.'

Anders must have died instantly as the weight of the cradle ground him down into the branches. Fletcher and Alvirez got the remains into a disposal bag.

'Carry him forward,' said Fletcher. 'We'll bury him on the beach and raise a cairn. This bloody copse is no place for a spaceman.'

The power module went along the last leg without any difficulty. They handled it with a kind of sombre ferocity. But it was as though the deity of the place had been paid its due.

At the end of the track, they hooked up in the usual order and Fergusson moved them out along the tongue. They were dog-tired. It was dusk, but the way was clear enough. By unspoken consent, it seemed agreed to get to a camp near the sea before the end of the day. The ground was almost flat. Occasionally, a shallow furrow jarred the springless axles. Gentle undulations like petrified dunes crossed the route for some miles. Then, before the last of the light had gone, they saw the line of the sea; a white luminescence across the violet darkness.

Dag Fletcher stood with Karen in the prow of the leading section as it bore them forward towards the beach.

He asked, 'What about tides?'

'Confused. Three moons. There isn't any detail. We may be the first visiting navigators.'

'We'd better stay well clear until daylight.'

A hundred yards from the water, he called down. 'O.K. Chad. Wrap it up. We're home. When you've finished dig out the trolley.'

Fergusson swung his trailers into the triangular laager and then disconnected the loading trolley for the last time. He and Myers lifted Anders from the back of the power module and put him on the platform. Then with Fletcher, Alvirez, Craig and Bennett—which was as many as could keep a footing on the small machine, he went slowly back to the last rise.

The vibrator excavated one foot square blocks of earth and stone, which they built into a simple pillar ten feet high, buttressed for the first five feet on either side by stepped blocks. Across the top line of the three block width, Alvirez incised with the tip of the vibrator:

CAPTAIN PETER ANDERS
INTERSTELLAR TWO-FIVE

followed by the date.

When they turned back to the ship it was completely dark. A pool of hard, brilliant light surrounded the laager. It would be visible for many miles in every direction. Fletcher wondered whether its value as a guard against surprise was greater than its danger as a wide advertisement. Karen said, 'I don't think it matters. They seem to know where we are without any trouble.'

As he agreed with her, he realised that the thought transfer bond was becoming stronger between them. Whether it was because of the deepening of the personal relationship or because some arrangement of forces on Pelorus was becoming stronger as they moved south, was difficult to decide. Probably the latter. Several times recently, he had caught himself anticipating what others were about to say.

A smell of coffee came in and he mechanically tested the air before taking off his visor. Also heat, like the draught from a furnace door. He looked at the suit temperature gauges and realised that there had been a steady build up. Here at sea level, it was fifty-one degrees Centigrade. It looked as though extra vehicular activity was going to be pretty limited later on. But just now it was still a relief to move in the open after the cramped confusion of the forest.

After the meal, Fletcher called a crew conference in the centre of the laager. He had a remote line from the recorder and began by finishing off the log for the day.

'Completing Day 50: Captain Peter Anders died this afternoon in the best traditions of the service. . . .'

Dag filled in the events of the day leading to the present position. Then he went on. 'According to Space Corporation Regulations, Co-Pilot Dag Fletcher automatically assumes command of *Interstellar Two-Five*. I ask now if there is any opposition in this full crew conference to that being so?'

He waited a full minute and looked round. There were half a dozen emphatic 'Agreed's. Smith, Myers and Craig were silent. Miranda, who had been more affected by Anders' death than anyone, was hardly listening to what was going on. This was her third voyage with *Two-Five* and she had come to the crew straight from the training wing. Anders had been unfailingly kind and helpful. She was genuinely sorry to see him go.

'Are any opposed?'

There was no reply. Fletcher went on, 'Thank you. That's settled then. In order to establish succession, in case anything happens to me, I exercise Captain's right and nominate my Co-Pilot, John Alvirez—if he accepts it.'

'Willingly. If the crew endorse it.'

'Is that also agreed?'

Once more there was general assent and no positive opposition.

'As far as the navigation section is concerned, its internal arrangements are, strictly speaking, no concern of the full crew conference, but I imagine there can be no dispute about Bennett replacing Alvirez as chief navigator?'

This time there was full assent from the only remaining fully qualified navigator.

Susan Yardley said, 'That's all right, Dag. Load everybody with gold braid and old dogsbody here will carry on with a twenty-four hour watch. Just throw a kind word now and again.'

'Don't worry about that, Susan. We'll all stay on the duty schedule. That's the end of official business. One thing more though. I don't know how this is affecting everyone, but some crew members are finding thought transfer links increasingly easy to establish. It may be we can use this as we go on. It may be we are moving into greater danger. We must watch each other and be prepared for group action against unusual behaviour. We are all experienced enough to know the need and accept the group obligation. Just as soon as we have a safety margin, we'll get Two-Five operational. Till then, there is no alternative, but to accept the hazards. The next stretch won't be too bad. Just a summer cruise. Is there anything anyone wants to put forward for the record?'

He looked round the circle of faces. They had all changed in the last strenuous weeks. Alvirez, Bennett, Smith had hardened up and looked very tough. Chad must have lost over fourteen pounds and looked better for it. Len Robertshaw looked more dour than ever. He was finding it rough. Craig and Myers had the spare build which showed least alteration but there was a harder line about them. The three women had put on short flimsy tabards and looked splendid. Karen particularly had a finer line of cheek and jaw which emphasised the classic oval. He received telepathically, 'Good luck in the command. You know my views.'

'Thank you. You look wonderful.'

Aloud he said, 'Meeting closed. We'll have the lights off and use infra-red. Dual watch duties in the control room.'

Alvirez stood with Miranda looking out from the bows of the command module cradle. With the lights off, a white thread separated itself in the distance. A slight movement of air brought a faint sea sound; as though small waves were falling on a shingle beach. The heat was stupifying. One of the small racing moons began its trek across the deep violet darkness. Talos was an unwinking red star.

Miranda said, 'Only salamanders can live further south.' As she said it, she shivered in spite of the heat. Alvirez turned her towards him. She was wearing a flimsy gauze tabard of fine, metallic mesh which, momentarily, felt cool against his skin. He put his hands on each side of her head and ran his fingers up through the thick, silky blonde hair.

Even the rising tide of purely physical feeling could not drown out a new mental power which was developing between them. Some adjustment of the manifold patterns of individual imagery was taking place. More than communication between two separate identities, it was an emergent thing, a common mind. It had an increase in complexity out of all proportion to the physical count of the double ration of cells and synapses on which it could draw.

Alvirez was aware of it in a tiny corner of consciousness which was left to him. The new common mind was moving out of the range of his single understanding. It was arriving at conclusions by paths which he could not follow. It was a computer which he had not programmed.

Then his lips came down hard and firm on Miranda's and her arms were round his neck. It was as though they were each resisting the responsibility of their own creation. Minds separated out into discreet units again, but left to them both was a sure knowledge. They knew without question that immense, intelligent force was being directed against them; that all the opposition they had met so far, even Anders' death, had been organised by it; that if they followed their present course, its power to oppose them would increase with every kilometre.

Later, he would talk to Dag Fletcher about it. But now, now there was only Miranda; satisfying all valencies like a perfect equation, with her perfume and the texture of her skin and her wide open, affirmative eyes.

CHAPTER SIX

DAG FLETCHER leaned over the side of the flagship, at the end of a measured twenty-five feet, and signalled to Karen in the bows. She dropped a piece of white painted log over the side and snapped down on a wandering switch which fed back to the computers. As the log passed him his arm went up again and she keyed in once more. He joined her as the computer finished its simple chore and gave the speed.

'Ten miles an hour.'

'That's a very unseamanlike unit. Len should educate his computers.'

'Haven't we enough complications?'

'Nothing hinges on great accuracy. Your charts, with all due respect, are very approximate. It's simply a matter of steering south until we see white mountains.'

Day 56 was calm. At this early hour it was possible to be in the open without a space-suit. They had almost completed a full twenty-four hours afloat.

The three small craft ploughed ahead in echelon with the command section in the lead. Although it had taken more work, each had been given its own propulsion unit, so that if the weather deteriorated, they could ride it out independently. Communication was by suit intercom since, in any event, the helmsman was now compelled to do his duty trick in space gear.

It had taken five days to get the cradles trimmed and bal-lasted and mount propulsion tubes. Chad had utilised subsidiary pumping motors to blast out powerful jets of water from tubes which swivelled like outboard motors and were rudder and propeller both.

Alvirez had incised *Santa Maria* on the bluff bows of the command cradle. On his own section, the cone, he had *Nina*. Bennett in the power module, completed the trio with *Pinta*. 'Just sympathetic magic,' he said. 'At least the first lot found land. Even if it wasn't what they were looking for.'

Personnel had been allocated so that there was at least one navigator in each craft. Fletcher, Fergusson, Smith and Karen were in the command module. Alvirez had Miranda and Craig in the cone. Bennett, Robertshaw, Myers and Susan Yardley manned the power pack. It made for a tough duty rota. Particularly in the cone section, where three-hour spells gave a maximum off-watch period of six hours, day or night.

Fergusson, as helmsman on the *Santa Maria*, called up *Pinta* and spoke to Susan.

'How does it go?'

'Well enough.'

'Steering all right?'

The swivel mounting was a simple pin and socket affair.

'It's a bit stiff.'

'The water will have made the wood swell. It'll wear easier. How's the cookhouse working out?'

'Galley, please. We have all the power we need. Fish today.'

Power they would certainly have on *Pinta*. Even shut down, there was a minimum, irreducible output from the massive motors, which had long since filled all available storage capacity. It was a pity that it could not have been used as a propulsion unit. Chad had toyed with the idea, but the only practicable plan would have taken months to implement.

'Fish?'

'Something like a coelocanth. Haven't you caught anything?'

'I'm in the wrong ship. Let me know if you have a crew vacancy.'

On *Nina*, Miranda appeared at the rear hatch and dropped lightly to the deck. As she went along the narrow catwalk by the side of the module, towards the bows, the ship swerved violently as Craig at the helm was distracted by her unself-conscious progress. She was wearing a very brief bikini which was bright blue in so far as it had substance enough to register colour at all. At the centre of the cone, she swung lithely up the stepped chocks until she could stand on top. Then she balance-walked along the curved surface to a flat section of heat shield. There, she spread a thick white towel and lay down. As an afterthought, she sat up, wriggled out of the token top and lay down again.

Fergusson said, 'Log that helmsman for steering an erotic course.'

At the chart spread, Dag and Karen considered the very sparse detail of the Polyphontine Sea.

'It's not much to navigate by.'

'I'm sorry it's the best I can do.'

'I'm not blaming you, Karen. You've done wonders with the material. As far as I can judge, we should miss Tragasus Island on this course. That means a straight bash for four-teen days and we should be in sight of the mountains.'

'What about John and Miranda's revelation?'

'I believe the opposition is sited on the plateau. We don't have to go as far as that. There is a narrow margin in our favour from anywhere up to ten degrees north.'

'But it can still reach us.'

'Whatever the power is, it's working at long range. There's a chance that we can reach a site for blast-off and still be far enough away. I've met this mental thing before. It's a matter of logistics like everything else. They have to concentrate enough power in one place. We have a chance.'

He went over to the port and looked out. The cinnamon sky was cloudless. Three white furrows tumbled out astern, fanning out to the horizon in the wine dark sea. Noise from the propulsion units came up on the tannoy as a steady hiss.

'This method of working is wasteful in good weather. At night we must arrange for one helmsman here and take the other two in tow.'

'It might be safer.'

She voiced what was also in his mind. It would be a guarantee that they all kept the same course.

Just after dawn on Day 58, Dag sent out a general call and signalled to Smith at the helm to cut power. *Nina* and *Pinta* had been taken in tow and came on until the three craft rocked together in a continuous line. It was still possible to spend the first hours of the morning without space gear. He stood in the stern of the *Santa Maria* and was able to speak to the other crews.

'We're making good time. I want a short halt here to do some checking. We've got planking working free. Take about an hour. Even if nothing's been noticed yet, it might pay to send a diver underneath.'

Alvirez and Bennett signalled agreement. Chad had already put on space gear. He hooked his line on a top rung and disappeared over the side. Minutes later, he surfaced and called for a zero reaction tool. Useful in space to exert a leverage where the operator had no toehold on substance, it was equally valuable under water.

After the long hours of motion and the continuous noise, the silence and change of rhythm made everyone edgy. It was as though the ships had suddenly become more vulnerable. Minutes dragged by. Chad was working along a whole seam, driving in pegs.

Miranda climbed to her sun-bathing station, took a short run, then plunged into the sea in a spectacular swallow dive.

Susan followed from *Pinta*. Craig and Myers were working on the undersides of their respective ships. There were no serious flaws in the construction. Pegs driven home now would make all secure.

On *Santa Maria*, Dag preferred not to leave Smith alone on deck. He stood watching the swimmers. Karen went in from the side with a controlled dive which hardly raised a ripple.

He called down, 'What's it like?'

'Hot bath.' Her hair was a dark copper sheath. 'Must be over 38 degrees.' She began a slow breast stroke round the ship. In the water, foreshortened, she had a sleek, rounded look.

Suddenly, the three boats lifted their bows to a small tidal wave and Dag spun round to look forward. Fifty yards dead ahead, still streaming like a half-tide rock was a massive, pearl grey, humped back. Even as part of his mind was bitterly reproaching himself for lack of forethought in letting the crews disperse, and for being, even then, more interested in Karen than in maintaining minimum security, he was racing down the catwalk to the entry hatch of the module.

Just inside, a small transmitter had been rigged to throw a relay on the main console. As the amplified alarm bleeps began to pulse out, the dome back was followed into the open by a long smooth flank like a surfacing submarine. Longer than the three ships put together, it lay across their bows like a barrier reef.

'Caught with our pants off, by god,' said Len Robertshaw from the tiller of *Pinta*.

Alvirez said, 'They don't give up, do they? If they can drum up one or two of these babies, we've had our lot.'

The three divers climbed in. Alvirez hooked his toes under a log for purchase, then bent over the side to take Miranda's wrists and pluck her out in one smooth heave. She shook back a mane of wet hair. Beads of water tinged with pink light stood out on her golden brown skin. Then she was off at a run to her cabin, followed, even in the emergency, by his appreciative Latin eye.

Susan was the best swimmer in the crew and had forged out like a torpedo for a hundred yards. Now she came in at a cracking pace which would have given her a place in an Olympic team.

To Dag Fletcher, watching the leviathan begin a slow turn to bring it head on to the ships, the return of the crew was painfully slow. In reality, it took under three minutes before everyone was accounted for and Susan, last in, had a hand on the lowest rung.

The monster completed its turn and lay, half awash, facing the ships. Below the dome of the head, jaws opened like the landing port of a car ferry. A slow movement like a sine wave progressed down its whole length and it surged forward. There seemed no doubt at all that it was looking for them. Now it had come up with its quarry it had to destroy it.

Dag was behind the flame-thrower on *Santa Maria*. The others were near enough to hear.

'Split up. R.V. beyond him. Get in a shot when you can.'

He signalled to Chad to get under way. *Santa Maria* began to turn to port. Alvirez dropped into the swivel seat on the cone and signalled to Craig to take them to starboard. As the mass in front of it began to separate, the ponderous head moved undecidedly left and right.

'A classic case,' said Myers. 'Balance the stimuli in every direction and you destroy the will.'

'Yes. There's a lot to be said for having a one-track mind,' said Robertshaw. Thereby, earning himself a warm smile from Miranda, as the stern of *Nina* sidled past them.

Bennett followed Fletcher. The Behaviourist School got immediate support. The massive head stopped hovering and began to follow the larger target. Not alone, the whole, immense body flailed forward. Chad fed every ounce of power he could get into the propulsion tubes and *Santa Maria* bucked ahead as if butted in the stern by a super-human goat.

Dag had been swivelling to keep a line on the centre of the dome. Bennett was masked by the other ship; but Alvirez had a target in the long grey flank. He and Fletcher fired at the same moment. Then Craig rammed in full power and *Nina* paid off in a tight creaming curve.

For a moment, there was a lull. The long grey shape had whipped under water and only a ragged swirl remained to mark its re-entry.

Then the world went mad.

The three craft made out on original course, still travelling at maximum thrust. Thirty yards astern the sea boiled with a deeper red and a grey and white tower reared out to a height of fifty feet. Strips of blubber hung like sails. The head gleamed white with streaks of skeletal bone. There was a roaring hiss like the escape of pent-up gas from a compression cylinder. Then it dropped back in a thrashing paroxysm of energy. A surging wave bore down on the lumbering ships.

Fatally, Craig looked behind him at the curving wall of water and his hands moved uncertainly on the tiller. *Nina* fell off a point and tons of hot water sluiced into the cockpit and foamed along the catwalk. The module hatches were above the surface, but the ship checked and staggered and thrust its bows down.

Alvirez fought his way back and cut power. Craig had disappeared. *Nina* wallowed sluggishly with decks awash.

Robertshaw and Fergusson had kept dead before the wave. The two ships lifted and tore along like bizarre surfboards on the crest. It was some minutes before it was understood what had happened to *Nina*. Leviathan was making its last, long dive.

Dag joined Fergusson at the tiller. Judging the moment, they heaved round together and the bluff bows of *Santa Maria* bit into the last wave. She came round with inches of freeboard and began to plough back. More slowly, the heavy *Pinta* turned and made for the other side. As they came up, *Nina* reached a point of stability with the lower part of the module awash.

Miranda's clear voice came across. 'It does prove a point. These things don't sink.'

There was no freeboard left. Pumping could not start until she had been lifted.

Dag said, 'Pass cables underneath. Then we'll move apart. Meanwhile, if you can spare Miranda, she can use the main scanner to do a grid search for Craig. One thing this under-lines. We need to close up the modules at all times. Get the seals on now, John, in case we capsize you.'

Light guide-ropes were passed underneath and then heavier cable until a web was drawn tight to support *Nina*. The two salvage tenders sidled round and brought the leads over the stern. Slowly they drew apart. For a moment it seemed likely that the whole after-deck of *Pinta* would tear away without any progress. Then *Nina* began to move. With an inch of freeboard, all available pumping gear concentrated on empty-ing her.

Miranda was patiently running down a square mile on the grid. Section by section she blew it up until a surfacing prawn would have shown. As the pumps sucked dry, she completed the final frame and came on the intercom link.

'No sign of Andy on the surface. But I've got a feeling about it. I think he's not far away. I can't explain this.'

Dag called John Alvirez, 'You'd better come across, John and talk to Cassandra. She's got a hunch.'

When he went through the hatch into the control room, Alvirez was instantly aware of something unusual. After the many weeks of travelling, they were all accustomed to the curious effect of passing through invisible bands of force. By a fluke, the control room was now centred in one. Either that or this was an exceptionally broad belt. Almost at once there was a build-up of mental cohesion. Without speech, he was aware of Miranda's thought that Craig was attempting to communicate with them.

They were both very still. Working now, deliberately, to enhance the mental link, he kept an arm's length away from her and tried to exclude from his mind even the eidetic image of her loveliness in the rudimentary, semi-transparent heat suit. She too made no effort to bring their private world into it. The common mind began to establish itself.

Its greater sensitivity was aware of Craig's thoughts. He was thinking in a cold verbal manner which was alien to their personal habits. Both tended to be mainly visual thinkers with words as a kind of running sub title. Craig was unconsciously sending out a disjointed sequence of phrases and sentences with little emotional overtone.

'Grass then. Weed of some kind anyway. What colour? Colour. Silver has no colour unless it shines by moderate use. Where did that come from? Something about a salt cellar. Sea's salt anyway. They'll look around on top. Not here. Get to my belt for a knife. Can't move either hand now. No knife anyway. Grabbed this suit in a hurry. Why didn't I float free? Must be some depth. All cats are grey. Every possible cat. My god, the strands are tightening. That's why. Not just weed. Some kind of anenome. That's it then. If I could use my hands I could open a valve and finish it. For God's sake get me out of here!'

Miranda broke in and the contact was lost.

'John. We've got to do something. Where is he?'

'Hold it, Miranda. I don't think we'd have got that if he'd been very far away. There's something stirring in my mind about this. The first time I ever knew what you were thinking about was early in the trek. You were climbing into the hatch and I was looking at your knees. Very attractive.'

For the first time, Miranda was impatient with a compliment.

'Get on with it.'

'You were directly above me. Now, Dag was saying that he and Karen got very accurate transfer when he was doing that balloon act. Directly above again. I believe there's particularly strong transfer in a vertical plane through any one point. Well a plane. Not necessarily vertical, perhaps. That could mean that he was directly underneath here.'

'Get Dag in.'

Fletcher said, 'It's worth a trial. From what you say, Craig hasn't got much time. It's a job for the power-suit. It will act like a bathyscope. Get Chad to rig a line on a harness and I'll go down.'

Four minutes later the robot suit was going over the side.

The prismatic eye in the dome saw the surface as a shining corrugated roof with the clumsy hulls of the cradles hanging in miraculous suspension. Dag dropped quickly, with a gentle rotatory motion. Pressure was not important in the immensely strong skin. It was a question though, whether or not they would have enough line to take him down.

At seven hundred feet the first tendrils of plant life swam into the beams of the suit's built in light. Flat, strap like, violet black with a paler underside, they ribboned out in the slight underwater currents. One tip touched his left arm. Others writhed towards him. When three bands had moved with uncanny precision to bandage the arm like a living sphygmonometer he began to tear them away with the free hand. Then he realised what Craig would be up against, in an ordinary suit. The tough fibres stretched and seemed to gather strength as they attenuated. Finally he took out a small vibrator from the external tool pouch and sliced them away.

The question was, how far down would he have to go? More tendrils were swaying out towards him. He seemed to be moving into a concentration of them. He called up Alvirez on the intercom.

'Any further contact with Craig? This is not good. Vision's

limited. We could be months searching here.' The circle of light was closing in; its perimeter a living wall.

'Nothing more. He may have been pulled out of direct line. Or it may be too late.'

'I'll go down another fifty feet. Then slowly up.'

'Check.'

Fibrous straps were coming at him from every angle. The vibrator gave almost instant clearance, but it was getting very dodgy. A gap in the black curtain showed up to his left. He used the suit's rocket trimmers to blast himself through and maintain him at the top of a pendulum arc.

Ahead, the plant had grown an excresence like a gigantic pod. In the second he reached it, he saw that it was slowly retracting into greater depth and he knew that he had found what he was looking for. The centre of the cocoon would be Andy Craig.

'John. Drop me fifty feet at a run. I think I've found him.'

Line went slack and, for a moment, he was sinking freely, controlling direction by short rocket thrusts. He reached the black chrysalis and began to cut it loose.

By the time Craig's mummy was half free, Fletcher had to take time off to cut away new strands on his own suit. He passed a line through the tangle round Craig and secured him to his own line.

He called the surface. 'You can take in the slack and begin a low power lift. As soon as I can cut free, we'll be coming up.'

When the black dome broke the surface, every crew member of Two-Five was watching for Craig's reappearance. Myers took a small vibrator and made surgically accurate incisions in the black carapace until the bronze suit was laid bare. Then the routine methodical chore of breaking out seals and Andy Craig was lying on deck, pale, eyes closed, but still breathing.

Myers said, 'He'll be all right. It takes a lot to finish a Scottish engineer. Somebody drop a penny and he'll be sitting up.'

'Let's get on then.' Dag Fletcher realised that full employment would be a good thing for morale. Craig had been luckier than anyone had any right to be.

'Use individual power for the moment. It gives us that bit of extra speed. Make up all we can before nightfall.'

The three small ships ploughed forward. The full heat of the day was building up and personnel on deck had to wear space-suits for their cooling systems. Only helmsmen stayed out. The modules with heat shields and heat dispersal ducting were keeping comfortable, so far, without any of the refrigeration plant being used. A squall of rain like hot blood suddenly beat down and passed. The air was heavy, oppressive, hourly notching up in vapour content.

Five days passed. On the morning of Day 63 Dag joined Karen at the helm of *Santa Maria* as the night tow was cast off and Alvirez and Bennett took over on their own propulsion units. As soon as he swung himself through the hatch to take up his duty stint, Dag sensed that something unusual was on the way. For the last two days there had been an increase in the trailing wisps of steamy mist which were a feature of the Polyphontine Sea. Now they were moving in a continuous bank of it. *Nina* and *Pinta* were phantom shapes, gliding behind a cinnamon-grey gauze.

In the silent, cotton wool world, there was nevertheless an uneasiness about the sea which communicated itself. A slow swell began to gather ahead. They rose to it and hurried on down the other side into a long trough.

'How long has it been like this?'

'It's developed over the last half hour.' Karen checked outside temperature. It was 49° Centigrade. She unsealed her visor and thick auburn hair spilled out over the neck rim like semi-liquid gold. After the stabilised suit temperature the heat was like a blast from an open furnace door.

Dag unsealed. 'We won't be able to do this very often now. In fact another two days should see the temperature getting up to sixty.'

'What kind of people can live in that?'

'People? Nothing hominoid. At least, any Earth organism would be sterile at that temperature. Something reptilean is possible.'

'But, after all, the actual physical form doesn't much matter. It's only a vehicle to support conscious intelligence.'

'Or unconscious intelligence.'

'Intelligence, I'd settle for.'

'Not for me. Intelligent life would simply regard us as a potential threat and aim to destroy us. It's the orectic side we want. The affective. The liking and caring.'

'You want to be liked?'

'An intelligence would see you as a hundred and twenty-five pounds of mixed human tissue, operating a primitive power pack and moving a potentially dangerous machine towards itself. Without stopping to consider the aesthetics of the matter and the fact that the hundred and twenty-five pounds are distributed in a very visually satisfying way, that at least two pounds, for instance, are arranged in silky, copper hair which has to be seen to be believed, it would seek to destroy you.'

'Which is what it is doing?'

'Yes.'

'So you think nothing we could do or say would be any help?'

'Nothing. All we can do is get to point X, assemble *Two-Five* and get out.'

Mist streaming past them pointed the build up of unusual wind force from dead ahead. A sudden strong gust tore gaps in the curtain. As far as the eye could see the horizon was notched and castellated by the dark shapes of the water against the sky. Dag said, 'Time you were in bed.'

'I don't want to leave you.'

He had taken her place at the tiller and she leaned over him until their foreheads were touching. As they came together, a sensitive, tingling awareness was common to them both. Speech was no longer necessary.

They listened together as the wind gathered and whistled through the tangle of chocks and frappings that held the module to its barge base. Timber creaked as the *Santa Maria* pitched down the steepening swells.

Bennett came up on the intercom. 'Not good here. I'll have to reduce to half speed. This power pack's very tender in a sea. Centre of gravity too high.'

Dag called up Alvirez. 'Hear that, John? We'll cut speed. Keep together. This could be a bad blow.'

'Check. What about an R.V.?'

'Usual thing. Look up this morning's course. Plot twenty ahead on the chart. Failing that, nearest land point. That's Tragasus.'

'Will do. Good luck.'

'And to you. See you.'

Before the mist shrouded in again, they saw that a white suit had joined Alvirez' bronze one at the tiller. Miranda had reacted to Alvirez' estimate of what was ahead and wanted to be with him.

With the weather coming from ahead, there was the best chance of riding it out with just enough thrust to keep them moving into it. More light, redder than usual gave streaks of illumination as the mist tore apart. The ships were only occasionally visible to one another.

Santa Maria heeled and sidled as crosswinds filled the troughs with a confused sea. Then she weltered about uncertainly, before picking up to meet the next swell. Down in a trough, the next wave looked like a hill moving down on to the ship. It seemed impossible that she would rise. When she did, the run down the other side went on until the bluff bows dug themselves in almost too far to pull free.

They were sealed up now. Standing on either side of the tiller. Safety lines hooked into shackles.

Wind force notched up another point. Steering error could roll them over. Calm in the troughs was followed by a furious battery of sledgehammer blows as they met the gale on the next crest. She was taking water and Dag brought in a hose line which used the propulsion unit for power and led from the bilges.

Heightened consciousness under the threat of danger made thought transfer easier than the intercom. Without speech he communicated a question about a new, irregular thumping which vibrated the planking beneath their feet. The reply, 'Module breaking free?' confirmed his own diagnosis. Somewhere forward the capsule was breaking loose, lifting and pounding down on its chocks.

'If it works free, it'll tear off altogether or dig itself a hole right the way through.'

'I can hold the course, if you want to take a closer look.'

It was like talking to oneself. He moved off, gripping hand lines which had been strung along the deck. He knew that she had used every ounce of strength to meet the next wave. Even a sharp pain, as her foot slipped on the streaming logs of the cockpit and twisted in a gap, was communicated. Then the range was too great and he was alone in the steamy, grey mist and sluicing water.

A wedge had carried away and the slackened frappings were allowing a six inch rise and fall. Each ship carried a number of spare poles lashed along the inside of the top strake. He worked his way along to the end and then had to hang on as *Santa Maria* came down into a trough and a mill race creamed along the catwalk. Then he was working to cut off a two foot butt with a small vibrator, bracing himself against the side of the module to keep inboard. Back against another torrent as they slid down into a valley and then he was twisting the lever into the slack rope and closing the gap.

Even as he bowsed it home and the module stayed locked on to its bed they were going up a cliff of water that defied description. Dag felt his feet sliding away from under him and he knew that he was almost vertically above Karen in the sinking stern. He was hanging on. It seemed that at any moment the module would break free and drop away from the barge altogether. Up and up. Then they were levelling out and diving at breakneck speed into the trough.

Now he felt his weight swinging the other way as the bows dropped away in front of him. They hit the valley floor like a plummetting gannet and the bows disappeared. The whole circular end of the module dug itself in and he was under water.

'This is it,' he thought to himself. 'This is the end of the line.' His mind was willing the ship to make an effort and heave itself out.

Karen's voice came crackling on the intercom.

'Are you all right?'

Before he could answer, he felt a new movement in the ship. Slowly, sluggishly, she was beginning to lift.

He said, 'We're doing fine. I'm coming back now.'

She was thigh-deep in water. With scarcely a foot of free-board, *Santa Maria* was wallowing along with the pump working overtime.

'Another one like that will be our lot. Get the feed pipes for the propulsion jet inside.'

The water level dropped at a visible rate and they took another roller without filling.

'We'll make it.'

'Why?'

'Every gale has its big wave; that was it. It could have taken us down.'

'I thought we should never climb out of it.'

'So did I.'

'Did you think of me?'

'When the chips are down, only the fight for survival matters.'

'I'm glad of that. I had no time to think of anything except holding a course. But I thought of you as soon as we were through it.'

'Thank you.'

Momentarily there was a glimpse of *Pinta* through a ragged gap in the pink-tinged veil. She was climbing a roller almost dead astern and about a hundred yards back. Very low in the water, with the lower part of the module awash. Dag hoped that the tripod legs, lashed below decks, had not carried away. Someone aboard her had seen them at the same time and an attenuated signal on the low-power suit intercom was marginally audible.

Susan Yardley's voice was just recognisable. 'We're completely waterlogged. No chance to pump free. Cradle breaking up. Must make for a landfall.'

Fletcher answered, 'Affirmative. Change course for Tragasus. Can you see *Nina*?'

'Acknowledge change of course. No sign of *Nina*.'

'Karen.'

'Still here.'

'Unhook yourself and get inside. Run a full power call for *Nina* on the main transmitter. Tell Chad about his good luck. Then get some sleep.'

The sea was still high, but most of the bite had gone out of it. Chad Fergusson's bronze suit made an appearance from the upper hatch and he climbed along to join Dag in the stern.

'I've left a robot call for *Nina*. There's no reply yet. Karen tells me you've been having a storm.'

He looked round. The mist had blanketted down again. Visibility was restricted to under ten yards in any direction. It was a closed in, crazy world of irregular movement. Fergusson went on, 'I'd like to get an aerial up and take a look at this. It's only a local thing according to the infra-red scan. About a square mile.'

'Arranged for us, you mean?'

'I hate to think so. This is control on a scale that makes us look silly. That's why I'd like to see the overall picture. It would give a clue to the method. They'd get the air in motion. Some cooling of the upper layers perhaps.'

Dag said bitterly, 'If Nina's gone they've been successful. One thing's for sure, we don't want to get any nearer than we can help. I'll settle for an attempt from Tragasus, if we can find a site that gives an even chance.'

'That is, if we find Nina.'

'One thing. They've made it clear that they won't let go. Even back at the first landfall, we were under pressure. We have nothing to lose. As soon as we land, Len can do some more calculating. We're a quarter ton lighter on personnel.'

The beginning of the long twilight found them within ninety miles of Tragasus according to the chart. As light levels fell, the mist darkened and lost its suffusion of colour. Suit gauges were showing 51 degrees Centigrade. It was a thick, hot darkness. *Santa Maria* was rolling along in a relatively calm sea.

Invisible, but on an audible link, *Pinta* struggled to keep going. Bennett called up, 'We're slowly breaking into scrap. I shall have to heave to.'

Karen, back on quartermaster duty, said, 'Check. I'll get Dag.'

She cut power herself and waited for him. When he came slowly through the hatch, he already had the situation in mind.

'Chas. We'll take you in tow. Get the tripod legs lashed to the module. It doesn't matter about the cradle. Take tow lines straight to the power pack. When it's set up, personnel come aboard here.'

Three hours later they were moving slowly ahead with Fletcher and Bennett at the tiller of *Santa Maria* and the waterlogged hulk of *Pinta* wallowing astern.

It was 0453 hours, Day 64, with visibility nil, when *Santa Maria* ploughed its bluff bows, with a kind of dogged finality, into yielding sand and *Pinta* came on to crash soggily into its newly halted stern.

Bennett said disgustedly, as he picked himself up, 'They've even moved the island.'

CHAPTER SEVEN

EXCEPT that there was a glow of colour in the mist, conditions of visibility were not better at midday, when the power suit dropped over the bows of the *Santa Maria* and sank into two feet of hot water and a foot of fine blue sand. Two strides took Fletcher to the water's edge and as much out of sight from the deck as if he had gone from Pelorus altogether. For the benefit of the watchers on the infra-red scanner, he stooped down and turned with two handfuls of dripping sand and said, 'I claim this land for the Spanish Crown.' Then he was lumbering forward, up a steeply shelving beach, sinking over his ankles at every step.

Binaural receivers kept the power suit on a line beamed from the console. This would give him a two mile straight run, like a dog on a lead. Without it, no certainty of return would be possible. Freak magnetic effects played havoc with compass bearings.

Sand gave way to a tangle of pale grey rock heavily veined with blue streaks. Twice he had to take the suit on manual control and move off the beam to get round obstructions, looming solidly in front with sheer faces lost in the mist three feet overhead. Then he was stopped by a solid wall which showed no break left or right for fifty yards. Further than that, he did not want to go, in case he lost the thin thread of the beam.

So it had to be up. He moved back until he was exactly in the beam path, and then the suit's extensor arm snaked away out of sight. It was some minutes before he was satisfied and then he retracted slowly. Fifteen feet up, the mist was thinning out. At twenty-five there was a horizon of half a mile. When he pulled himself over the lip and stood upright on a broad ledge of blue grey stone, he was in the characteristic cinnamon light of Pelorus, looking down on a sea of tinted cotton wool mist which stretched away indefinitely in front of him.

Peaks of blue grey rock showed up like islands, heat shimmered off the wall at his back. He turned round again and faced the cliff. Only about twenty feet remained, unless there was a further ledge, and he went on. At the first attempt to lift, the edge crumbled away and he dropped back. Then it held firm and he was on a uniform level platform of rock which ran back for a hundred yards before it gave way to the most fantastic jungle he had ever seen.

Immense cycads, trees that soared with smooth clear boles like Corinthian columns to improbable heights, ferns, flowering shrubs and festoons of purple lianas melded in a rioting kaleidoscope of every colour in the spectrum.

One thing was certain. There would be no moving through it. But the platform he was on had distinct possibility. Len Robertshaw could run an analysis of the take-off data. Stripped down to the bare shell, they might do it. Then he remembered the cone. But the decision stood. He would go on as if he had a ship. Rebuild it here as far as they were able. At worst they could live in it until their power gave out.

There was no question of living outside. Suit temperature gauges ruled that out. A man would hardly survive twenty minutes without heat protection. And be a hospital case at that. Dag took in a sample of local atmosphere. The hot jet of air carried with it a heavy bouquet of overripe vegetation. Foetid, fecund, like standing beside a mountain of half-rotten germinating seed. 'Goat Island' was about right.

A heavy shower of warm rain streamed down on him and ran, half an inch deep, on the slightly tilted rock. It made an instant Niagara over the cliff edge, then stopped as suddenly as it had begun. Half a minute later the rock had steamed dry and was baking in the cinnamon light as if there were no water in the world.

Dag picked up the beam and began to retrace his steps. Going down into the mist was like a move into some under-world. Without the thin thread of the beam, human isola-tion could go no further and remain conscious. This would be a Kafkaesque setting for illusion on a grand scale. The sooner they were out of it the better.

Len Robertshaw went through the data with more than his usual painstaking thoroughness. Dag's estimate of height was not good enough and Bennett made the trip up with a portable navigation set to bring him a pinpoint, positional fix in three dimensions.

It was 2000 hours before he was prepared to make a state-ment and then he said, 'Look, Dag. I know what you want me to say; but I can't say it. Statistics are my profession and I can present these to give you the answer you want. But I've never twisted the facts yet, and I'm not going to start now to ease anybody's conscience. This is for certain—given the position and the weights and the power reserve as stated, it is possible to create an escape velocity. Possible. Just. Any one of a dozen imponderables would tilt it the other way. Safety margin is virtually nil. In any circumstances other than these, I would have to come out in definite opposition to any proposal for lift off.'

'That's fair enough, Len. I appreciate your analysis. I know exactly where I am with it. The decision is mine and I'll take it. We go on. We'll assemble the two stages on the plateau and look for the cone. When the time comes I'll put it to the whole crew and get their views on the record.'

'That's your prerogative as Captain. You know you have my support whatever line of action you follow.'

'Thank you, Len. I rely on you. We haven't had the last of the mental infiltration yet. Keep us on this side of sanity.'

Chad Fergusson spent the next day devising lifting gear. Working with the trolley's winch and the power suit it would be relatively simple to make the two stage lift up the cliff face. The cradles could be winched forward to the foot of the rise. It was just a matter of applying what power they had. By the time Robertshaw had made his report, it was too late to start and the only preliminary move which could be made was to disentangle the power module from its disintegrating cradle and haul it on two skids above the water line.

In the command cabin, Susan Yardley lay back on an acceleration couch and followed the weaving, delicate intricacies of a Mozart symphony. The scanner on infra-red was set for repeating circular sweeps which brought in the beached cylinder of the power module every twenty seconds.

After the long strain, it was difficult to let go. Karen woke at the end of a short, uneasy sleep and sat up in her narrow bed. She shook back her hair and sat for a few moments, elbows on knees, absently twisting a long auburn strand round her fingers; a habit which she had carried from childhood. Then she swung her legs to the deck, stood up and stretched with a sigh. She wanted to push aside the walls and get out. She wondered if it would be possible to walk on deck even for a few minutes without the drag of space gear. The idea moved her to the door and she was sliding it back when she remembered that she had discarded even the light sleeping tabard. No prude, Karen was realist enough to know that she was disturbingly beautiful. There were difficulties enough. So she turned back and slipped into a thin blue zipper suit with heat insulation disks.

To conserve refrigeration, they were using the space exit lock. That would give her an idea of what it was like outside. If the incoming air was too hot, she could go back.

In the next cabin, Dag heard the slight noise of her movements and was instantly wide awake. He registered that the footsteps were going towards the exit lock. It was just after midnight, Pelorus time. Watch changed in an hour. Susan on duty. That should be all right. But he found he was too wide awake and uneasy to sleep again. Resigning himself to follow a sixth sense, he began to zip himself into the silvergrey space-suit which hung ready beside his bed.

He was going down the corridor to the lock when alarm bleeps sounded their urgent warning.

Susan had picked up Karen on the scanner as she came out on to the catwalk. She saw her shiver as the heat blast stimulated hot and cold nerve buds alike. Then as she turned back evidently deciding that the great outdoors was no marvellous catch, a thigh-thick, writhing, black and green tube slid out of the mist and clamped round her waist like a monstrous arm. Susan's reaction time was phenomenally fast; but even as the bleeps began, Karen was lifted to the side.

Dag came out of the lock as the arm retracted and drew her into the mist. He took the side in a clumsy running vault and came down in water up to his chest, beside a shaft of bony crab leg which stood in the mist as though it had independent life. As it began to drag itself upwards, he realised that the foot was deeply embedded in the sand. It had been standing there for some time, close in to the side waiting for a victim.

After a brief blaze of recognition that he was near, Karen's mind had ceased to communicate. She was out or dead. The arm he had seen would have no trouble in breaking her back.

The Laser was useless; shooting into the mist was as likely to drill a hole through Karen as anything else. He snatched out the vibrator from its clip on the front of his harness and cut deeply into the slowly moving leg.

The vibrator needle could make its way through most hardened steels. Organic matter opened in front of it as

though it were parting the air. The severed leg fell away from
him and half a ton of mottled, grey black shell loomed out
of the mist to bear him down into the water. As he went
under, he had time to pull the toggle which beamed a small
built-in torch from the chest gear of his suit. In some ways it
was easier to see in the water than in the mist and he caught
the blue gleam of Karen's suit. The trunk had relaxed its grip
and she was being pressed down into the water by the falling
body. He was able to grab her hair and a handful of blue
material and push her free. Then the creature was grinding
him down into the sand.

The weight was intolerable, the flexible ring construction
of the suit resisted pressure to some extent and the water reduced force, but a residual dead weight of a quarter ton was
driving him into the soft sand bottom. Fighting for every inch,
he moved his fingers to the lanyard which carried the vibrator.
By the time he got to it, he felt that only seconds remained
before his heart burst out of his chest. When his fingers
closed on the handle, he no longer cared whether he cut into
his own suit or not. Anything to end the intolerable torture.
As far as he could control it, he directed the needle in an
upward twist and pressed the activator.

Momentarily, the pressure on him increased, as the creature
gained purchase to lever itself away from the biting blade.
He must have blacked out for some seconds, because his next
impression was of feather lightness, as if he were under par-
tial gravity, and he was standing free with his visor above
water.

Nothing was visible except the reflected light from his own
torch making a small white dome in the mist. Then on the
perimeter of its circle, strands of dark copper floating towards
him.

Seconds later he was holding her head above water and strid-
ing for the shore. Only patient elimination of possibilities
would find the ship. Now that he knew the direction of the

shore, it had to be left or right and not more than ten yards. He tried the way it ought to be and in five strides the bows of *Santa Maria* were standing out in the mist.

The whole action had been under three minutes and the alarm bleeps were still sounding through the module. Bennett was climbing down in the power suit and handed Karen up to the deck, where Susan was at the lock ready to take her inside.

When Dag had peeled off his suit, Susan had been working for two minutes with mouth to mouth respiration. He took over, almost at once her eyes flickered and then opened wide. A residual horror cleared with relief and breathing began to stabilise.

Dag said gently, 'Let me know next time you feel like lobster pas de deux.'

Her eyes were wide open with dilated pupils and her mind was a blank parchment. He could move in without reservations. Instead, he put down his own barriers and made a conscious effort to blank transfer areas, so that she was forced to pull together her own organisation. Then she became a personality again and he was aware of her gratitude, that he had respected her rights as an individual. His mind told her that he would only ever take over when it was willed consciously by both of them.

Myers was waiting to run a medical check. After a brief inspection he fished two capsules out of the medical bag and put them on the tiny dressing table shelf.

'Nothing wrong that sleep won't put right.'

Then he was out and they were alone together. Dag took the capsules and drew water from a water tube.

'Take these like the man said.'

In spite of efforts to control it, her hand was shaking too much. He put an arm round her shoulders and held the thin silver cup to her lips.

'Don't go until I'm asleep.'

'Your hair's still damp. That fire ball is a great help. It identifies you in a mist.'

She was too drowsy to rise to it. Then she was asleep. One thing was clear. They were still under surveillance. Moving up the cliff would be a tricky job.

Action was the obvious antidote to the dispiriting effect of the mist and the unknown threats overside. Ven Smith was going about with a set sombre look. He was the living model of a man biding his time. Myers was with him constantly. Robertshaw, always independent, had little to say to anyone. Chad Fergusson had taken Susan across to the power module to dig out some necessary stores. Karen was still asleep. Fletcher and Bennett were at the chart spread, where they had eaten breakfast, since the extra personnel overcrowded the facilities of the tiny navigator's wardroom.

Smith caught Myers' eye and they left the wardroom. Robertshaw did not even look up from his chair. He was listening to a library tape on an individual earpiece. Outside, Smith said, 'Along to your cabin. You're the medical man; you can prescribe a drug.'

When they were in the small dispensary, he went on, 'What about our "do or die" commander, now?'

'He's welcome to it. We should have stayed on the other side.'

'What do you prescribe?'

'There's nothing we can do. We'll have to go along with it.'

'I don't know so much about that. With Alvirez gone, the next in line is Chas. Bennett. Now he's not a bit particular about these heroics. If Fletcher goes we have a man of our own mind.'

'And then what?'

'Either stay put on top and run a robot distress signal on 1420 or take the power section back until it's cool enough to live outside. There's enough power there to last a small group a hundred years. Take Karen and Susan. They'd see it our way, given time.'

'Chad Fergusson wouldn't like that.'

'I'll look after the engineering side. You can deal with communications. Susan's a navigator. Basically, that's all we need.'

'Basically is right.'

'Keep your eye on the main chance. Rewards handed out at the end.'

'There should be some opportunities on the move. Anyone disappearing in this mist has had it for a start.'

'There'll be a chance. Don't doubt it.'

In the power module, Smith was losing a potential element of his plan. Susan was working closely with Chad Fergusson in the narrow confines of the Engineers' Stores and something which had been building between them for some weeks was reaching a definition. Once in the module, they had removed space gear to expedite the chore. They were lifting rolls of cable from narrow racks to get at long lengths of line stored beneath them.

Short dark hair, falling straight to the delicate line of the jaw, athlete's figure, slim, almost as tall as Chad. Ribbed, moulded inner suit of pale yellow. Grey eyes rather wide apart. They lifted a roll of line, which proved unexpectedly heavy. Her side dipped and only quick reactions made him able to balance the load and lower it down without dropping it on her.

'Sorry Chad.' Wide, grey eyes looked into warm brown ones. Moved by a common understanding, she stood still and waited for him to step over the cumbersome roll. Then his left arm was round her shoulders and his right hand drew her supple thighs firmly against him. Their lips met slowly and gently.

Susan said, 'I'm not very good at this, Chad. I haven't been interested before.'

'There's all the time in the world, Susan.'

A faint crackle from a suit intercom drew them back to the object of the exercise.

Fletcher's voice was patiently repeating the standard call for attention. When he finally got it, he said, 'As soon as you can, Chad, there's a lot to do.'

What was to be done had to be done slowly and with infinite care. After Bennett had lost himself for a good hour, like an arctic type walking round his tent in a blizzard, they each hooked up and ran out on the built-in exploration lines. It made for safety, but it reduced speed. Dag used the power suit and Fergusson had the loading trolley. They moved the two modules to the foot of the cliff by applying overwhelming force and dragging them on rollers. The rest of the party walked alongside and fed rollers to the front as the rear end left them free.

The cargo winch from the freight hatch of the power section easily lifted the command module on to the half way ledge. Dag had cut bollards in the living rock to take the line. Then it lifted itself. Without a continuing rise to give height, the next lift was more awkward. But working in daylight was a pleasure in itself and Chad produced a rough tripod support to take the block and tackle.

Working flat out, it was 2100 hours with the light almost gone and the cotton wool sea turning violet black, when the command module came to rest on the plateau.

Ven Smith had had a bad day. The most reasonable locale for his attempt had been the first leg to the foot of the cliff. But no opportunity had presented itself. He was prepared to drill through the power suit with his Laser, but self preservation was strong enough to hold him back from the slim chances that were offered. He knew that Fletcher would not miss if he bungled his shot and some sixth sense seemed to be directing him to keep the broad back of the power suit out of danger.

One opportunity knocked and he prepared to take it. The power pack had begun to winch itself up the first pitch and Fletcher was under it, using the power of the robot suit to ease it out from the wall and cushion its impact with a soft log buffer. Smith was waiting at the ledge to catch the first appearance of its end through the mist and fend off with a lever. Chad was working the freight winch. The others were preparing lines to take the command module further up. Cutting the line would send the heavy power pack falling free, with a force that would crush even the robot suit. He leaned down over the edge and reached out to touch the rope with his vibrator. A second would have been enough. But with inches to go a heavy hand on his shoulder was heaving him back.

'Watch it, Ven. You're getting too keen. You'll be falling off the beetling crag.' Bennett had either not appreciated what he was going to do, or was in favour of the action, but not the timing; because nothing more was said. Probably it was the former, because the vibrator needle held on the underside of the gauntlet was not easily visible from above.

One last task seemed worth the effort to Dag before wrapping it up for the day. He went down to the ledge for the flame-thrower, which was still attached to the power module. He reckoned that whatever the jungle contained was likely to be on a big scale. If any of it was given to wandering out on to the rock to sport by moonlight, they might be glad of all the armament they could get.

The command module had been stood on end and ready to be lifted into place on the first stage when the gantry had been rebuilt. Before settling it down, Dag checked the site with a primitive inclinometer. He was coming round to the view that whatever the force bands might be, they were not good and it would be just as well to be clear of a direct path. There was a heavier concentration on the plateau than they had yet met, but there was a twenty-yard belt which was free. That would do for now and for the ship when they assembled it. It was necessary to mount the two guns on the circular lid of the sixty foot high cylinder. Access to them would have to be through the internal hatches which meant a considerable loss of refrigeration every time they were opened.

Then they were all inside and Chad was filling sheets of scrap paper on the chart spread with diagrams of a gantry simple enough for their unskilled hands to build and yet strong enough to sway the fifty ton cone over a hundred and thirty feet up to its resting place. If it was ever found.

He said, 'Look Dag, I believe I was the one who had the idea that the cradle timbers could be used again to make the terminal gantry. It was a good comfortable theory. But I'm not too sure about it now. They've taken a hammering over the trip. There's no heart left in most of that wood. We need a stiffening of new material and there's a whole forest full over there. I suggest we pull out half a dozen top size vegetables to make the main members.'

'O.K. by me. You're the expert. First thing tomorrow. Correction, second thing. Get the power pack up and then do it. Site the gantry about where we are; I don't fancy being too near that lush spinney.'

Light from the module made a clearway to the edge of the vegetation and lipped out over the cliff edge. In the middle watch, Karen Evander sat at the chart spread, hatching in more detail on the route plan. If it ever got back to the Pilotage Centre it would more than double the available information about Pelorus. At intervals, she checked on the scanner picture, roving in endless panoramic sweeps along a hundred yard frontage of jungle and through three hundred and sixty degrees.

Nothing moved. Meticulous to the last detail on a duty stint, she switched in the outside microphones to check noise level. There was none. The audiometer registered nothing.

This was so unusual that she looked up the instrument check panel expecting to find that it was signalling an equipment fault. But apparently the recorder told no lie. Noise level was nil. That was odd. On the previous checks it had been normal. The sort of high level mush that could be expected from a super tropical forest.

A rain squall swept down and the needle flickered up, justifying its maker's optimism in its reliability. Then it resumed its negative position.

Half in, half out of consciousness, a vague worry was formulating. She resisted it, thinking that the experiences of the last twenty-four hours had left her nervy. She took the scanner on manual and subjected the jungle frontage to an inch by inch scrutiny. The fantastic conglomeration of shape and colour was a camouflage in itself. Anything could be there. It was like looking for a concealed object in one of those children's puzzles. Except that in this case one did not know what the object was. So the pattern-seeking mind had an impossible task.

Naturally enough, she had made a first sweep along a band to a height of fifteen feet. She recognised it as an assumption that could be wrong and came back up to thirty, then forty-five. Taking it through to sixty was the sort of attention to detail which had filled her personal file with 'A' ratings.

A patch of fork-toothed, green foliage, thirty-one degrees left of centre on the hair-line markings of the screen was showing an outline, so incredible that, for a moment, she believed it to be hallucination. Solid patches of a deeper blue green filled in behind the discrete leaf shapes. The pattern was pieced out by half-forgotten memories of high school history tapes. A massive, gaping, reptile head. Then it was gone.

For a moment, Karen felt panic. Perhaps it was imagination. Simultaneously she realised that she must react as if it were true. It was better that she should look foolish than that she should overlook a real menace. She flipped in the alarm key

E

and made another slow traverse on the forty-five to sixty feet band.

Len Robertshaw, who had made his bed in the computer room to solve the accommodation problem, was first in.

'What is it, Karen?'

Before she could answer, Dag Fletcher and Myers were through the hatch. She turned to Dag. 'There is something, Dag. A reptile head. Almost sixty feet from the ground. It's there.'

There was an undertone of anxiety in her voice which was a plea for reassurance. He ignored Myers and Robertshaw and held her tightly. A muscular tremble in the upper arm belied the calm, professional manner.

He said, 'Every member of this crew is still here, because over the years their colleagues have checked on the outside chance. This is far from unlikely. It seems to take our well-wishers about a day to adjust to what we're doing. The timing would be right. I believe they follow us by some communication through the varying force bands. The whole planet is a chequer board. If we're sensitive to those currents, it's not impossible that some resident has developed ways we can't imagine of using them for communication. And control too. They could be the vehicle for mind control. Remember, Dan Munro's amplified music programme sabotaged the system. Working on that hypothesis it would be easy to direct any animal governed by a brain, however marginal, to move in a certain direction. Every time it passed through a force band it would get the message. Repetition of stimulus at more than the likely frequency of chance would be enough to orientate it and keep it moving. After all, that's the statistical basis of all thought.'

He was deliberately talking to take her mind off whatever it was that she had seen. The jumpy muscle had already knocked off its pas seul. Before she could reply, Myers said in an awed voice, 'Holy cow, Theropod Tyrannosaurus.'

Susan was the last member of the crew to assemble and came through the hatch looking preoccupied. She heard Myers and asked before she looked at the screen, 'Is that bad?' Then she saw it. 'Don't answer that.'

Nobody moved in the control room. An immense reptile, with nutcracker jaws open in a mindless gape, had pushed its way from the fringe of the jungle and was standing on the open rock. It was erect. All of twenty metres, from the tripod of claws and armoured tail to the petrified wattle which protected its pea brain.

Myers put the scanner picture to record. This sequence would make the biological report a best seller. He said, 'The biggest flesh-eating dinosaur of the lot.'

A minor hurricane seemed to hit the jungle perimeter. Feathery tree tops bent down and lashed back. Two more reptiles came out. The confusion spread deep into the jungle. Dag spun the traverse and the picture ran along the frontage. Every fifty yards or so, to the limit of its range, there were more of them. It was a concerted move.

They were clearly uncertain of what they were to do. Some were tearing at the massed foliage, which had closed again, like a curtain, behind them. Two had begun a ponderous, menacing, circling manœuvre which was a prelude to courtship or total war. Some began to shuffle forward. Any one of them could push over the sixty foot canister of the module and roll it off the edge of the cliff.

Dag said wearily, 'Here we go again. Chad, come upstairs and operate one of your blow torches. Positive group thought from everybody else. Remind this lot that history is on our side. All the light we have.'

From the top, they were roughly level with the heads of the reptiles. The pool of light, which spread out as soon as they had made a record change into space gear and climbed out through the top hatch, showed more than a dozen reptiles whose almost random movements had brought them dangerously near. Dag took the nearest. The brilliant light gave a ruby glitter to small eyes as its head weaved from side to side. Small, embryonic forearms dangled like empty sleeves. It was beginning a casual walk towards the capsule.

At twenty yards, Dag sent a searing lance of flame into the open jaws. He emptied a whole charge in a slow dropping shot which petered out half way down the bulge of its chest. Its upper works virtually disappeared. Main nerve centres were so quickly and completely destroyed, that the vast remaining bulk settled motionless like a grey bulbous trilith.

Then it was in motion again. But this time it was being torn to pieces. The two nearest dinosaurs moved with more animation than any had yet shown and turned on the corpse with an explosion of violent force. A rain squall drenched down and the water ran red.

Chad fired. It was sickeningly easy to kill. Then Dag again. The area round the module was becoming a fantastic shambles. More theropods were coming in from further out along the jungle wall. The pattern was the same. Each one that fell occupied several others until it was torn to quivering pieces.

Then one dropped and was ignored. Those nearest to it still came on and Dag realised that a new instruction had been got into the midget brains. They were to keep going. Now it was more difficult to keep the space clear. But it had to be. The barrels were so hot that new charges were spontaneously discharged as soon as they were fed into the breech. But targets were too big to miss.

Still they came, clawing a way through slippery mountains of charred flesh.

Chad said, 'I'm getting low on rocket charges. If there are enough of them, it can only end one way.'

'There are enough.'

Fletcher began to call up control, pausing to make further sweeping shots. Finally, he got Bennett.

'Send up the reserve rocket charges.' After some minutes of silence—'No spares. More down in the power pack.'

'In that case, we have about ten minutes before this tin can gets booted over the cliff.'

The estimate was over generous. With a shot that settled an oncoming monster back on its heavy tail, so that its remains slowly toppled backwards away from him, Chad finished his quota of charges.

Fletcher had time for a bitter reflection that his leadership had brought his crew to useless and unnecessary death; then he was preoccupied by a concerted move as four theropods cleared the obstructing mounds and came on towards the module.

He used his last two charges in a traverse which encompassed them all. Then he stood clear of the flame-thrower and took out his Laser. There was needle accuracy in this weapon and the fine beam would drill through any known material; but finding just where a needle hole would do most good in a reptile of this size would require more research than time would allow.

Below, half-way down the module, the lock began to open up and the power suit came out. It climbed quickly down the retractable ladder and reached the ground as new arrivals began to force their way through the debris. Only when it was in sight from the roof did Dag appreciate what was going on. In reply to his question, Karen's voice, clear and determined came back at greater strength on the robot's high power transmitter.

'I've been thinking over what you said about the force lines. It's a chance that we can transmit on one as well as receive. Their control at a distance may be no stronger than our transmission at close quarters.'

The suit was fifteen yards out. Overshadowed by the massive flank of a defunct theropod. She went on, 'I can get the message too. There's a definite feeling of compulsion to turn and move towards the capsule. That's what they must be feeling.'

Fletcher was down through the hatch and making for the lock. The nearest theropod was twenty yards away when he came up beside her. He said, 'Nice work, Karen. Relax and think about us. Think together. Together.'

The emergent mind began to grow between them and use its greater power to work something out to save them. They stood together. Rain rushed down, beating off the suits in bright rivulets. Their individual minds felt a wavering of forces and then a cessation of the compulsion to go towards the ship.

CHAPTER EIGHT

BENNETT had been calling for some time before his voice, on the intercom, penetrated their private world. When Dag dragged what was left to him of an individual mind to the task of replying there was an edge of anxiety in Bennett's tone.

'Whatever you two are doing out there, you can stop doing it. They're all going home.'

Watchers in the control room, where the whole crew had spent the night in an uneasy vigil, saw the two suits, dwarfed by the monstrous gobbets of theropod, begin to pick their way towards the ship. Outside the force band, they stopped; and Fletcher's voice was normal and assured again when he called up for Myers.

'What's the position, Ralph, on the biological front. There's decomposition here already. Do we need to follow full decontamination drill?'

Myers replied, 'I'll run a test. Hang on for a few minutes.'

Full procedure would hamper movement over the next few days. Once a ship got its biological seals on, it was a painfully slow business to get in and out. But if it was necessary, that was it. Certainly they had no facilities to sterilise the outside area over a wide enough field. Whilst they were waiting on the small platform of the lock, Karen said, 'This mind business is frightening. I don't object to losing my mind to yours; but it could be anybody's, couldn't it?'

'I don't think so. We were half-way there to start with. I *wanted* to know what you were thinking. But a formidable mental machine could be built up by a whole group of human brains willing a corporate activity. Could be very dangerous. Somehow, I don't think that's happening here. This mental force is powerful, but not as overwhelming as it would be. It may be a united effort by a large number of relatively simple organisms, which might have no individual reasons for opposing specifically human forms. A group mind based on human units would have known what we were doing.'

'But we have passed hominid cultures.'

'Hominid. Not human. That small gap is still the biggest step that evolution ever made.'

Myers cut in, 'Sorry to interrupt the sweet talk, but decontamination drill is definitely on. As of now, we shall have to sterilise every external surface which comes inside as we build. Final outside cleaning will be automatic when we get into solar heat.'

'All right, Ralph, spare us the long-term gloss. When can you take the power suit?'

'Right away.'

Karen was reluctant to go.

'You must be tired out. And this is one occasion where you can't insist. Physical force is on my side.'

The outer iris eye of the lock door was opening up behind them. Turning as though to take her offer, Dag brushed close to the chest console of the power suit. Before she fully appreciated what he was doing, he had slipped the setting control to *Outside Manual*. Then foiling every attempt she made to alter it, he levered the heavy suit back into the opening. When she was in, he said, 'Strength maybe, but not guile. See you in half an hour.'

He looked out over the littered table of rock and began to plan out the moves that would take them to the end of the day.

After two hours stand-down and then a breakfast session which was taken in unusual silence, they were ready to begin.

The thought of the extra drag of observing biological sealing drill was enough to account for it. Coming at the end of a long voyage and a hard, dangerous trek, it was an inconvenience, petty in itself; but felt to be the last straw. Dag privately registered admiration for the records official who had selected and balanced the crew. John Alvirez and Miranda Dolon would have transformed the situation. If the full crew had been meeting the difficulty, it would have been discounted. But even forethought could not anticipate a precise casualty return and put spare jokers in the pack.

The robot rendezvous call was going out ceaselessly. It was geared to trip a relay and bring in a general alert if an answer came back. There was no joy. Dag could not believe that the cone had gone down. Alvirez would have sealed it up before the storm. But it could well be floating without its cradle, anywhere in a hundred mile diameter circle. If the cradle had gone, probably Alvirez and Miranda had gone with it. Craig could be alone and without motive power. But there were communications systems in the cone. Any one of the three could set up a homing signal, which would be a beacon even in the mist. He would have to fit out some kind of craft from the remains of the two cradles and make a search. But the immediate task was to get the ship together as far as they could.

It was important to get everything out in one go. Re-entry was now a time-consuming chore. Chad Fergusson had prepared a detailed inventory and a mound of stores blocked the narrow corridor behind the lock. Then they were out and securing lines to the power module to bring it up.

The site for the reassembly of the ship was near enough to the command module to make that section useful for the tackles which raised the power pack on to its tripod legs. Working without a break, they reached that point of reconstruction by 1400 hours, Day 66.

E*

Ninety feet tall on its tripod, the business section of *Two-Five* dwarfed its neighbour. The crew rested in its shade. Even the few degrees advantage were a help to the hard pressed cooling systems. Chad drew four circles on the rock, each one lying on the quadrant of a circle which would ring *Two-Five* at a distance of three feet.

'I want excavations here to take the boles of four trees. Ten feet down should do it. Then we'll cross-brace at intervals with short lengths. It can stay in place for lift off. If we can't go straight enough to miss it, we can't go straight enough to get away.'

Dag said, 'All right, we'll get on with it. There's only one vibrator big enough to go through those tree trunks, so we'll need it on the lumber party. It can be sent back as soon as the trees are down. Meanwhile, Karen and Susan can make a start with hand vibrators.' He had been standing close to Len Robertshaw and even in the unusual light of Pelorus, he could see that the older man's face was grey and strained with fatigue.

'Len, I'd like you to get inside and run an intensive search as far out as you think reasonable. We need news of the missing section. Then get things ready for us to come in. We'll take another two hours and call it a day.'

The remaining five men loaded the big vibrator on to the half track and picked their way through the decomposing remains to the edge of the jungle. At close quarters it was clear that, this time, there would be no easy way to get the trees they needed. Only the power-suit could force its way through the prolific, spawning tangle of plant life which fought its way out of the teeming ground into the steam heat.

Chad Fergusson, as the most experienced operator, was currently in the robot. He went forward at a slow walk and the massed foliage gave way in front of him. Two strides, with the suit developing its maximum horsepower, forced back immense fronds with thigh thick, resilient, triangular section ribbing. Then he disappeared. Bennett and Smith, who had moved up behind him, were flung to the ground by the flick back.

'That's all we need. Get at it Myers.'

Before the two had regained their feet, Fletcher and Myers were slicing at the bland, unbroken vegetable wall. Progress was slow, even when the four were working on it. Two feet were enough to show what had happened to Chad. The rocky edge rimmed a swamp as abruptly as in some laboratory vivarium. Peat, like a soft full sponge, was the jungle floor. Probing with a rough spar showed a firm bottom at about six feet.

A small convulsion seized the tropical paradise in front of them. Then Chad heaved himself out. Black slime ebbed away in thick, glutinous ropes; bands of broken weed trailed behind. Leeches like tennis balls clung to every possible surface of his suit and to the vibrator which he still carried.

Bennett said, 'My god, it's the Queen of the May.'

Fletcher said, 'Come on, Chad, don't mess about; there's work to do.'

It was two hours of patient work, before the first tree fell on the precise line that had been planned for it. The robot suit and the half-track dragged it back until its massive bole was pointing to one of the excavations. At this rate the gantry would take a long time to build; but there was no other way.

After checking with Robertshaw that nothing new had come up on the scan, Dag drove his team back to the timber yard.

One thing he was glad to note. The force bands seemed to be free from any discernible message. No new compulsion was throbbing out to send a fresh wave of attackers against them. Well, that was a good thing as far as it went. But it was utterly unlikely that they would be left alone. Two bands of force crossed the clearing on the way to the jungle edge. He stopped deliberately in one. Apart from the slight sensation of moving into an indefinably different light there was nothing to register.

The next log took an hour and a half. He determined to bring three in and then break for the main meal. After that they could come out and get one more and then call it a day.

When the long trunk lay pointing to its ultimate site and Dag said, 'To coin a phrase—once more into the breach,' there was a moment when Smith debated whether or not to make it an issue. He was sick to death of the whole business. He was standing near Myers and plugged himself on the personal link. 'What about it, Ralph? I could drop Fletcher from here, before he knew what was going on. You take Fergusson and we'll be sailing out in a week.'

An older adage than he knew about was justified again in Myers' hesitation. Myers thought about it and the moment for effective action passed.

When the third tree was lying in place like an immense spoke, one excavation was complete and a second one had been taken down to four feet. At the day's end, every one of the eight was ready to drop down and sleep where he stood. The biological cleansing drill was the last turn of the screw. Discipline carried them through it. But the set faces that gathered in the Navigators' Ward Room were a warning to Dag that he couldn't expect them to keep going at that pace.

Part of the trouble was lack of defensive armament. If he had only the minor weapons of an I.G.O. corvette, he would have been independent of any physical attack which could be mounted by any organism on Pelorus. There was certainly a case for reviewing the charter and allowing arms on civilian ships. Certainly 'freight and exploration' vessels like *Two-Five*. Then he would have been able to take reasonable time over the rebuilding.

He was looking out of the command cabin window at the four main structural members of the embryo gantry when Karen joined him.

'Satisfied with progress?'

'What progress?'

'Don't be like that. We're all working like beavers.'

'Sorry. I'd be more content if I knew where the cone was.'

'Haven't they got one of the small weather balloons?'

'Yes. So?'

'They may be getting our R.V. signal, but they wouldn't, necessarily, be able to reply. Miranda's a top-rank specialist on communications, but she hasn't any workshop facilities in the cone. We have a wide visual field of search. Suppose we send out a signal asking them to send up their balloon. It would act like a marker buoy over the mist.'

'Alvirez is no slouch. He'd have done that if he could.'

'Not necessarily. He'd assume we were in the same mist. He's not to know that it's low-lying.'

'Could be. I'm only arguing to convince myself. It's a good move. Of course we have to try it. Len can get a message on a circular tape and leave it bashing out.'

He manœuvred Karen towards the hatch. The animation of explaining the idea had taken some of the strain lines out of her face. But she was plainly very weary.

He said, 'The thing that puzzles me is how anyone who looks so beautiful can be so clever. It's very unfair. Bed. There's another long day coming up.'

'What about you?'

'I'll come in to say goodnight in about ten minutes. There's something to lay on with Chad.'

The relationship between them was without tension. Each felt the other to be an extra dimension of the self. The awful burden of individual consciousness had temporarily ended for them.

Working with the heavy vibrator, excavation was speeded up and by midday, Chad was satisfied. Reinflated, the blimp was anchored to one end of the first trimmed trunk to be moved. Then with the freight winch and the trolley hauling, and the power-suit and the blimp lifting, it was eased along until it fell into its prepared niche. There it was steadied and wedged with rock slivers, until its two hundred feet were plumb-line straight, in a soaring pinnacle beside the ship.

Hot rain squalls had sluiced the remains free from blood and the putrescent mounds were grey green. It was like working in a macabre slaughterhouse. Moving occasionally through the nearer force bands, Dag became conscious of two things. There was no overt message now being carried through the medium; but any delay in moving through resulted in a kind of mental discomfort. Pain would be too extreme a word to use, but he was glad to move out. Smith, working with him on a shackle round the massive trunk actually cried out and ran for it. His face was twisted in a grimace of agony. Two yards down the trunk he stopped and clearly the pain had gone.

The other thing, which was less positive to determine, was that the force bands themselves were not stationary. There was a slow drift. Whether this was a natural flux or a directed one, it was impossible to say. But certainly, in three hours, the point at which the leading edge of the band crossed the tree trunk had altered by about a yard. A drift towards the ship, then? Dag kept the discovery to himself. It must be slow because even after three days the building site was still in a free zone.

He marked the trunk before they stopped for a break. An hour later the front had crept forward another six inches.

By the end of the day, the four uprights were in position and Chad was using the balloon to lift him in the power-suit to the points where notches had to be cut to take transverse beams. The crossbars themselves could be lifted in by the same method. It was like working with a very docile elephant.

Checking pegs in the rock, Dag found that the movement of the band was irregular. For some hours it would drift back.

But it always resumed its slow approach to the ship. Presumably it would go on beyond it. Unless some controlling agent stabilised it on that place.

Karen got to know about it in one of their sessions of communal thought. Her individual reaction was that, among the many hazards, it was only a marginal one. The joint mind made no communication about it, though they were aware that it had been considered. That in itself was strange; that the emergent mind should be keeping matters away from its component units.

The second work session of Day 68 saw the command module lifted into place on the power pack. Now the top platform was just over a hundred and forty feet from the rock and *Two-Five* was looking more like a ship.

The section settled into its locking collar with micrometric accuracy. Smith, hanging from one of the gantry poles and wearing the power-suit moved it delicately as it fell slowly through the last inches to marry up the guide slots, which would automatically bring every one of several hundred male and female couplings in line. Then it was done and he was aware that the tide in his affairs was at a flood which might never occur again.

The only men in the ship were Len Robertshaw, who could be discounted as a physical force, and Ralph Myers, who was there to complete the biological seal as soon as the sections were joined.

Chad was working the freight winch below the power capsule. In these conditions of biological security, this compartment was isolated from the ship by sealed hatches. Susan Yardley and Karen Evander were tailing on a steadying line with Bennett on another at an offset angle. Dag Fletcher was standing well back and conducting the orchestra with a combination of hand and voice signals.

It was a fair chance. As soon as the couplings clicked home, he was going up the next twenty feet, to the opening of the lock, on the extensor arm of the power-suit. The flexible chute from the platform had been retracted for the move; but even if it had been in place, nobody could have reached the lock before him.

Recognition of some menace in the move came belatedly to Dag Fletcher as he saw Smith disappear into the lock and the iris eye of the entry port began to diminish. With the biological drill to go through, nobody went inside except to stay.

He called the group, 'That looks a lot better. All we have to do now is find the top bit. Send the chute down, Smith. We'll have an early night.'

The answer from the power-suit was loud and clear. Smith was still occupied with the elaborate decontamination procedures. He called Myers, 'Ralph, this is it. Get along to the control cabin and take over from Robertshaw. Cut that signal for the cone and we'll suspend the distress call for the time being.' Then he went on to spell it out for the group below. 'Two-Five stays where it is. And you stay outside. Any time Karen or Susan want to opt in that's all right. Otherwise they can spend the rest of their brief lives telling you how clever you are to bring them to this place. The main vibrator is inside here. Don't try to get in.'

Fletcher said, 'Smith, you're signing your death warrant. You'll never get away with it. You can stick it out in the ship for a year or two with luck. Then you've had it. There could be an I.G.O. patrol on the way in now. There are some log entries you can't erase and won't be able to explain. Open up now and I'll report extenuating circumstances.'

'Thank you *Commander*. You can stick your report where it will do most good. In twenty-four hours you won't be in a reporting mood. I'm switching off this net, so you can save your breath.'

'Smith, you damn fool,' Fergusson broke in, 'what do you

think you'll get out of it? You're worse off without the group.'

There was no reply.

Fletcher said, 'Leave it, Chad; he's not hearing that.'

The five had gathered below the freight hatch, where the mass of the ship gave shade and suit gauges dropped to fifty-six Centigrade. There was a general attitude of unbelief. The ship had been their home and the focal point of their life for so long, that it was hardly credible that they should be excluded from it. The longer term implication—that to be denied its reserves of power made them victims of an environment which they could no longer control—was not on immediate issue.

Bennett said, 'Assuming we all followed regulations and drew reconditioned cells this morning, we have about three days—give or take an hour or two.'

Fletcher said, 'I have to put this to Karen and Susan. If you go inside, there is a chance that you might find a way to take back the ship. In any event, there is no point in dying out here. You have a duty to preserve your life as long as possible.'

He resolutely closed his mind to its memories of what Karen looked like inside the anonymity of the silver space suit. He said harshly, 'I order you to accept the offer.'

Karen said, 'Thank you for making it easy. Whether you log this or not, I will not obey that order. It isn't, believe me, just a matter of the physical thing. Apart from the fact that I love you and want to stay with you, whatever happens, there's the matter of professionalism. If Smith had said he wanted a cartographer I might have gone. If you hadn't been here, that is. But the role he has in mind, I fill only on my own terms.'

Susan had moved over to Chad Fergusson. She spoke more to him than to Fletcher when she said, 'I agree with Karen. You don't get rid of us as easily as that. This is the hazard we all accept—every time a ship lifts off. This time we lose.'

The long twilight of Pelorus was setting in. Periodically rain squalls swept the plateau. They had been three hours standing and sitting in the space between the tripod legs of the ship. It was going to be a test, to destruction this time, of their powers of boredom tolerance.

None of the external machinery, fed by power from inside, was working. Smith had obviously made a thorough check. Fletcher and Fergusson had climbed the gantry for a hundred feet to test the lock entry. All outside controls had been disconnected. They carried on to the top platform. Again the hatches were secured, so that they could only be opened from inside. But the flame-throwers were still there and one box of charges. It was the obvious place to spend the night.

Chad took half an hour remoulding the acceleration couches which had gone to make the swivel seats.

'Since they flatter us by choosing our company, we must make them as comfortable as possible.'

When the two girls would only accept the beds on a strict rota basis, he gave it up.

'What's happened to those sweet and biddable women who only live to please?'

'They never were more than a legend.'

It was an uncomfortable night. Dag had occasionally spent longer in the confines of space gear, on missions during I.G.O. service; but the rest had not done so since training wing days. The knowledge that it was an endurance test which could only end one way was no help either. This time the long Pelorusian night seemed interminable.

The small moons made their orbits in turn. No light came from the ship, though no doubt Smith would have the scanner working on infra-red. In the violet black darkness, the stars were coloured stones on a velvet cyclorama. It was like the vigil of priests on the summit of a ziggurat. Small wonder the ancients were preoccupied with astral lore. Dawn showed up in streaks of pale green and lemon-yellow light. It contributed nothing to the hostile landscape; but it was psychologically welcome. Another day. Day sixty-nine. Dag wondered if Smith would continue the ship's log.

No one had slept much. Even the spell on one of the cradles had not easily brought rest. They had worked a long session on the previous day without a meal and they had been more than ready for food when Smith made his play. Now they were all hungry. Water was no problem. It was a by-product of the energy cells and small amounts were always available in a reservoir inside the visor. Biological waste was chemically destroyed and could be disposed of without breaking atmosphere seals.

Heat and light increased together. Dag said, 'Time to move into the cellar.' They used a stirrup loop and lowered themselves hand over hand on a running fall. When they were standing once more on the rock, he said, 'If Smith keeps his nerve, we can't get in. If we wait here, we surely lose. We have already lost valuable time. I have to apologise for that. We'll move back to where we can live without this equipment. At least, we'll start in that direction. There's the blimp here. We can make a light cradle for it. It will just about lift us and some of this gear. Then we can drift north. Fly north, if Chad can devise an airscrew for the trolley motor. The sea's full of fish. In twenty-four hours we can be eating it.'

'In this outfit?' Bennett was not leaping about with any show of enthusiasm.

'There's a slight temperature drop over the sea. Enough to make it possible to open your visor for a few minutes. Don't you want to eat again?'

'O.K. O.K. You've talked me into it. When do we start?'

In the full baking light, Smith and Myers watched the figures begin to work on the clearing. For some time it was not apparent what the object of the exercise would be. When the half-track was weighted and its winch began to haul down the balloon, Smith got an inkling of it. He looked thoughtful.

'That bastard Fletcher is very artful. They're going ballooning.'

'There's nowhere to go.'

'I don't know about that. They could drift back over the sea. Get hold of food even. In the long term it won't do them any good. Perhaps we ought to do something about it.'

'Like what?'

'Like blasting a nice big hole in their balloon.'

'What about Len?'

'He can stay in his cabin. He can't get out. He's no man of action. It won't be long before he's thinking along the right lines. If not he can go out.'

Myers put on an 'official report' voice. 'The acting captain, Fletcher, was killed with the rest of his party whilst attempting a balloon survey of the area. At this stage in the voyage, this can only be described as an error of judgment since it left the ship without adequate personnel to organise a blast-off.'

'Very neat. Very neat, indeed. And it gives me a thought. Where's that balloon now?'

Myers brought it into the picture. It had been wound down until its silver, dolphin back was level with the closed freight hatch.

'Better than a big bang just now. A number of small holes to bring it down a few miles from here. If they stay here, desperation may drive them to do something foolish.'

He dropped down the companion ways to the bulkhead above the freight hatch, where he was on the same level as the balloon. A narow tube in a ball joint gave access for a small mechanical grab, used to collect earth samples in a situation where the crew could not leave the ship. He began to disconnect it;

then remembered the biological seal. There was plenty of time. He left the last screw plug in place and went up one deck to the engineer's wardroom to call up Myers on the intercom. Let the expert see to the seal.

By the time he was ready to fire a thin Laser beam down the tube, the party below had completed a rudimentary cradle with the trolley as the main part of a base platform. Smith's engineer's mind was working out some rough estimate of rates of escape. He finally came up with the view that three Laser holes would be about right. With some feeling for the aesthetics of the situation, he placed them in a neat equilateral triangle and then left Myers the delicate job of completing the seal, whilst he himself returned to the control room to tune in on the Bosch landscape and watch the final preparations of the toilers in the pit.

Working from a vague memory of a paddle device to move an elementary balloon craft in the dawn of aeronautics, Chad had mounted roughly trimmed blades directly on the winch spindle. Making adjustments by trial and error, he believed they would hit on an arrangement of angles to give enough thrust to move them along. There wasn't, in any event, much choice.

Dag said, 'There's nothing to keep us here, as soon as you like, Chad.'

'I want enough rock chippings to ballast the cradle. Then we can pitch them out to get height.'

As they rose slowly up the side of Interstellar Two-Five they were able to look in at the control cabin port. Smith turned from the scanner and gave an ironic wave. Something about his manner troubled Dag. He would have expected Smith to see their move as a possible threat. Remote perhaps and unlikely, but just barely menacing. He looked too confident that they would not succeed.

Then they were rising to the rim of the top platform. The two flame-throwers were lying beside the couches. He called

Chad. 'Hold it there for a minute. We'll take one of these equalisers. In any case the charges could be useful.'

The extra weight slowed the rate of climb. Bennett finally cast free the land-line altogether and they drifted up another hundred feet. Chad made an adjustment to the plane of his paddle blades and then fed in some power. Drifting stopped and they began to move purposefully over the ground.

'What course?'

'Due North.'

'Or any necessary compromise?'

They began to sort themselves out in the confined space of the cradle. There would be just room to stretch out one at a time on the floor. Sleeping would be by rota. For the rest it was a matter of sitting round the low parapet rail, hooked on for safety. The action of the last hour had done something to take their minds off hunger, but now it came back at full strength.

The point of their original landing on Tragasus Island must have been part of a deeply indented bay, because a northerly course kept them over the land. Below them the rocky plateau narrowed as the swamp pushed out to the edge. Where it finally spread to the limits of the rock there was a smooth, unbroken flow of water in a mile-wide Niagara. From above it seemed motionless, as though a plastic moulding was leaning out from the cliff. The lower edge cut the mist, which curved into it like the under belly of a cumulus cloud.

It was impossible to tell where the coastline lay. The mist could cover land or sea. They were moving along parallel to the cliff edge. After the falls, the ledge broadened again until the edge of the swamp had receded several miles.

Chad said, 'We're losing a bit of height. Heave out a medium sized rock, Susan.'

Another convoluted twist in the land below brought them above the jungle. The cradle was only twenty feet above the tallest trees which pushed out like islands in an impenetrable sea of vegetation.

Bennett said, 'I'll be happier with a bit more height. The way things grow round here, we're a fair mark for any enterprising snake.'

'I can't quite make this out.' Chad sounded genuinely puzzled. 'There's no reason why we should lose height. Heave out some more rock.'

The blimp felt the decrease in its load and went up another fifty feet. But there was a lack of buoyancy about it that was unusual. In all the work with the balloons, they had become used to having them move up like an express elevator. Half an hour later they were back again with the cradle picking its way between the taller elements of the jungle floor.

Susan said, 'That's the last rock. Now it's like that game where you have a doctor and a sociologist and a musician on a raft and one of them has to be put off to save the other two. Whom do we throw to the sharks and why?'

Fletcher said, 'Now I know why Smith was looking pleased with himself. I should have checked. He was able to fix the blimp. Small holes I expect. I've played this right along the line he wanted.'

'Don't blame yourself. It was a reasonable line to take. We all agreed and still do.' Karen had a gauntletted hand on the corrugated arm of his suit. A wild swing of the cradle made a moment of confusion. Only their superb reaction times kept them all inside. When the violent pendulum swings stopped they were missing the general level of the tree tops by less than a foot.

'Cut the drive, Chad. We can't stand many snags like that.'

Without forward motion they lifted a foot. There was a slight drift east of north. Each mind was adjusting to the possibilities. Movement below was virtually impossible. It looked very like the end of the line.

Bennett said, 'We're gaining height.'

There was four or five feet below the cradle. Then it was ten. Karen said, 'I don't think so. The vegetation is lower. Not quite so lush either. Some draining of the swamp. Of course, that's it; we're moving back towards the falls.'

Torn ragged holes in the blue green carpet looked down into outcropping stone. When the cradle finally lodged where it would remain, they were a hundred feet above an irregular cube of dark grey rock. It was a small island in a sea of slime.

Beside the stone a long blue-black form moved amongst the broken camouflage patterns of foliage. Then it was gone. Noise level was intense and Susan, who was very sensitive to noise, turned down the outside mike on her visor.

Dag Fletcher was eaten up with a cold, consuming anger. His mind refused to accept this as the end. The incredible skills and knowledge represented in the group could not end here in two feet of primeval slime. Looking at Karen's silver suit, with its trappings of a millennium of scientific progress, he saw also the beautiful body inside it. With an effort of will, he shut his mind to everything but action, and his voice on the intercom was a harsh snarl which bit through the apathetic silence.

'Get a rope down, Bennett. Move man. We'll go on on foot. We'll work back along the coast to the hulks. The *Santa Maria* will still float and the propulsion unit's still on it. We'll *sail* north.'

Nobody said that the time left in the suits would hardly get them to the coastal strip. Or that they were feeling too weak to move. Or that the force bands were carrying a rhythmic pulse of power which beat into the brain until its balance was on the disturbed edge of screaming lunacy.

Chad dropped down first into the dark hot liquid beside the rock. He reached a firm bottom standing waist deep and steadied Susan as she came down beside him. Fletcher came

down last, with the flame-thrower tube across his shoulders.
When he reached dead level, he gestured forward.

'This way.'

They began to struggle through the hot clinging slime.
Suit gauges were registering well inside the red quadrant at
a steady sixty-five.

CHAPTER NINE

TIME meant nothing, place was an indistinct, semi-liquid, shifting, formless pit; neither light nor dark. Consciousness was awareness of pain. In rare moments of lucid thought, Karen knew that she was mechanically following the rope that led away and disappeared in front of her. Each one on the five bead chain was alone.

Sometimes she knew that Dag Fletcher was in front and Susan somewhere behind at the end of the line which went back into the elemental chaos. More often she knew nothing. Only the pain of the gathering heat, which her suit mechanism could no longer neutralise. Weakness, hunger, and, when they crawled agonisingly through a force band, the frenetic beating of a rhythm which destroyed every pattern of thought and reduced the minds to a million individual needles of torment.

Fletcher went on, because his mind was locked on the single consuming aim of going on. He no longer knew why he was moving or where he was going. Sliding, clawing, crawling, he went forward. When the line behind him went taut and Karen was lying face down motionless, he went back and drummed with clenched fists on her closed visor, until the devil's tattoo penetrated into her dizzy brain. Then he lashed her with blistering invective that shocked her on to her feet and made her begin stumbling steps towards him. Then he was away again and she was alone in the world of instant agony. He became the author of all the evil that was besetting her. She

wanted to kill him. As she clawed her way after the disappearing rope, she began to search in her belt pouch for a
Laser. She would kill him and then the torment would have
an end.

They had been moving in the swamp for seventeen hours.
At first there was a pattern in it. Two hours move, one hour
rest. Now there was nothing.

Dag Fletcher was hanging free, spinning at the end of his
unbreakable rope, washed by a torrent of water that slid over
from the edge of the swamps. The change in light and sensation was just another dimension of illusion. He fell jerkily,
foot by foot as Karen was dragged nearer the brink. It was
not until his feet had found a stop on the ledge behind the
water, and the rope went slack as his weight came off it, that
a moment's clarity told him what had happened. Then Karen
was coming down, silver suit washed clear in the warm flood,
twisting as he had done. Looking about her with an arm
stiffly bent. Looking for a target.

He flattened back against the rock face and chopped the
Laser out of her hand. It fell away silently into the curtain
of water. She grappled with him using all that was left of her
strength to send him after it. Then she went limp and he
propped her against the wall and turned his attention on
Susan, who was drawn on, by the inescapable logic of the
link, to follow down.

Through the visor, he could see her white, set face. Eyes
closed, lips pressed in a pale line, jaws rigid. She could be
dead. The rope behind went slack then Chad came down in
a free fall. Fletcher had time to throw himself down beside
Susan and their combined weight brought him up short at the
limit of the ledge. Then the following rope snaked down. It
was unbroken. The toggle at the end had been unsnapped.
Bennett had opted out.

Minutes ebbed past. Fletcher regressed in an offbeat phase
of illusion. The zombie figures of his crew gyrated on the rim

of a clock face. The sickle hand was coming up to twelve and the figures receded from it on another plane. How could the hare catch the tortoise? In the time it took the hare to reach the spot where the tortoise had been, the tortoise had moved on, however slowly, to a new place and so on through infinitesimal gradations for ever. His mathematical mind jibbed at the old fallacy and he focussed on the dim underwater world of the ledge.

Chad was pulling himself painfully to his feet. Susan was a white blur on the spray-swept floor and Karen had slid down to sit with head bowed forward on her knees. Infinitely weary, he said, 'How does it go, Chad?'

'Just.'

Perhaps it was imagination, but it seemed less hot. He looked stupidly at the heat gauge and it was some minutes before the numerals meant anything. It was lower than it had been for many days. Some vacuum effect behind the fall possibly. The reading was 49.

'Chad.'

'Still here.'

'We can switch out refrigeration. Give the cells a recovery period.'

'What refrigeration? Mine packed in.'

'Stay here. I'll be back.'

There was no way of knowing which would be the nearer limit of the waterfall. Chances were even. Dag was facing the wall and went left. The ledge was narrowing and the slope of the face thrust out until water was breaking its smooth line on his shoulder with a force that threatened to wash him off. He went along sidestepping with his face to the wall. The ledge was down to nine inches. Then six. A projection would have pushed him out into the fall.

Then the liquid filter was gone and heat bit into his back like a lash. A yard away, the broad ledge began again and he shuffled along to it. As he turned round the heat built up and he fumbled for the switch to bring in the failing cells for some relief.

Out in front, the pink-tinged, cotton-wool sea stretched away indefinitely. Somewhere below it was the coast and the sea and the boat they would never reach. Almost dead ahead and about half a mile distant one of the small moons of Pelorus was stationary.

He moved his head and then looked back at it. It was still there. Belatedly, recognition came to him. It was a small weather balloon. Alvirez must have got the message. The cone was down there. A spell of dizziness caught him unawares. The balloon was below him and the fleecy sea was a low ceiling sky. He was grovelling face down on the ledge, holding on as the vertigo insisted that he would fall backwards, like a loosened tile from an upside down roof. Fall under gravity. Gravity an expression of the geometry of space time. His mind caught hold of the definition as it flew past, a straw in the wind. It began to ravel back associated ideas. Runaway gravity implosions. People on earth would double in weight if distant stars were wiped out. Interdependence of every fragment of every galaxy to the limits of comprehension. His mind found a toe hold in abstraction and began to stabilise itself, until his cramped grip relaxed and he felt the rock steady underneath him.

On hands and knees, he looked again. It was a weather balloon all right. He estimated that it was rising from an anchorage point on or near the coast. He thought of going back, then he knew that he would not be able to make it there and back and then on, with the others to force on. In any event, they would be better waiting where they were.

If the depth of the cliff were much the same at this point it would be well within the length of his coupling line. He looked round for some anchorage point and slowly hacked out a recessed socket to take the hook. Then he put the ratchet on and rolled himself over the edge. The friction pawl adjusted itself to a one tenth gravity fall, but, unco-ordinated as he was, the jarring crunch as he hit the level left him winded and unable to move. Finally he heaved himself to a sitting position and put his back to the rock. There was nothing to be seen in the clinging mist. He was no longer sure of what he was doing or why he was there. He was a tiny fragment of life in an alien void. The unconscious took charge. He detached himself from the hanging line. He began to crawl away from the rock.

John Alvirez found him by making semi-circular sweeps at the end of a long line; tethered to the cone like a goat. Miranda had picked up the mush of crazy signals from his intercom on the receiver she had improvised from the few materials available in the cone section. At first, she believed that some feed-back in the circuit was making a gobble out of the background static. But the rhythm of it was like a kind of speech and she tuned on it with great care.

'John, there's somebody out there. Not far either. It's speech on an intercom mike.'

'That's service. The balloon hasn't been up half an hour yet. That doesn't tie up though. Why would they cut the R.V. and emergency signals before they made contact? They went out as if they'd given up. And that's not like Fletcher either. He'd go on with that signal until he'd found us or he was sure we'd had it.'

'You think something's wrong at their end?'

'Sure of it. They were very likely in the same mess that we were. But the two sections must be in contact or there'd have been a call for the power pack as well.'

'I'm getting it again. It's not far away. You'll have to go out and have a look.'

'Look? You're joking, of course.'

'I tell you it's very near. Hook up on a line and work round in an arc.'

There was no doubt that she meant it. Alvirez had been

ready to follow Craig's example and take a spell of sleep; but he began to set up his gear and do the routine checks which were as much a part of life as breathing for space personnel. They had drifted to land with the cone clear of its cradle and floating tip down almost two thirds submerged. When the wooden shell finally disintegrated they had been hooked on to the tumbling capsule and dragged along with it in individual chaos until the storm dropped to a sullen swell. Then they had hauled in and climbed aboard the reeling metal platform. No direct intervention in the course was possible. They held on, glad they were both still there.

Then it was calm enough to risk opening a hatch. They dropped through into a scene of shambles and smash, where Craig was making half-hearted efforts to sort the place out, believing that there was no point in it, that indeed, he would be the only survivor and that he would drift in the cone until the power gave out.

When the tip of the cone grounded on soft sand the sway continued almost unchanged and it was some time before Alvirez realised they had made a landfall. They edged further in until it was possible to take lines ashore and heave up to a secure mooring. Then Miranda had begun to work on a basic receiver with a bigger range than the intercom sets.

Moving through the force bands, they had registered the changing messages that they were carrying. But their landfall was in a clear area and Alvirez only met the fragmentation rhythm on his second sweep. When he was through it, he called Miranda. 'There's a new thing on the force network. If the ship stopped in it, this could be the answer. Anybody who couldn't get out would go crazy.'

'I'm not getting that voice signal. Whoever is out there with you has gone silent.'

'Thank you very much.'

It was on the next sweep as he was hurrying to get out of a force band, gritting his teeth against the pulsing rhythm

which was destroying the electrical balance of his brain, that
he fell over the prone silver figure, which was as invisible
as his own feet in the cotton wool mist.

'Miranda.'

'Lord?'

'What's that?'

'I said, "Lord". Flattering your ID.'

'Don't mess about. I've found Dag. He's in bad shape. Rouse
Craig out at the double and get him here.'

'I'll come.'

'Look. For some reason, I only trust you at my back. I want
you where you are, so that when I knock, the door will open.
Get it? Now do as I say and get Craig out here.'

'Check.'

It was typical of Miranda that she accepted an explanation
without argument. It was also typical that Craig was dressed
and finding his way along the line that led to Alvirez in a
time that would have beaten any Training Wing record. Together they lifted Fletcher and worked back by shortening the
rope.

Passing through the force band was slower with the lay
figure. Craig was hardly conscious when they stumbled out
of it. What sort of effect it was having on the man they were
carrying was anybody's guess.

When Dag Fletcher opened his eyes in the cool, stabilised
atmosphere of the cone, Miranda was holding his head whilst
Alvirez was forcing a thin bitter draught between his clenched
teeth. His overheated, reddened skin had been bathed with a
corrective for mild burns. If this was death it was a change
for the better and he was all for it. He was probably in a
minority of one in thinking that Miranda's honey-blonde
head should have been auburn, that, in fact, she shouldn't be
there at all, but somebody else should be leaning over him
and putting him back with a restraining hand as he tried to
sit up. That focussed his mind on where Karen was and he

remembered the ledge, though where it was, he did not know. His voice sounded immensely distant to his own ears as he said, 'They're on a ledge, underneath water. There isn't much time. Karen, Susan and Chad. Bennett's had it. Follow the rope up the cliff.'

Miranda said, 'Well, you can hardly miss a cliff. There's plenty of thin line, leave yourself a trail.'

'Thank you, Ariadne.'

The first trip took over an hour. They brought Susan in first; because when Alvirez finally toed his way across the ledge, and found their improbable resting place, she was clearly the furthest gone towards the point of no return. After that, it was more straightforward. Chad came in last in thirty-five minutes flat.

Miranda said, 'Glad to see you, Chad. It all goes to prove that old maxim about survival of the fattest. What would you like to eat? We can put on any kind of vegetable soup. You name it, I've got it. You're right in the heart of vegetable country.'

Even after its buffetting, the cone section was still in business as the fresh food farm of the ship. There were no other supplies, but the hydroponic tanks could come up with an endless stream of green stuff. Given time they could grow corn for bread, but at the moment Miranda was experimenting with thick soups.

Outside, they were getting the phenomena of the day's cycle even at the bottom of the blanket. The mist was dropping by shades into an opaque violet black. Inside, Dag was making his way back to the operational strength.

He said, 'God damn Smith to hell. He's loused this up properly. We'll be lucky if we can muster a viable crew. If Len's gone, you're on your own in communications, Miranda.'

Miranda said nothing. She sensed that Myers had been counted off strength and that it would be tactless to quote him.

F

Fletcher went on, 'We're strong on navigators, but we're short on anything to navigate. The sooner we get moving towards the ship the better.'

Alvirez had been visiting the wards. He said, 'Chad's coming on very well. Karen and Susan ought to rest a couple of days before they do any mountaineering.'

'It'll be all of that before we can move. We can work along the coast to the old cradles. One of them is seaworthy and has its propulsion unit. Bring it back here and then move the cone up. From there, we're in striking distance of the ship. Then we work out how to get inside. As far as Smith knows we're all dead.'

'What about the balloon?'

Dag slapped his forehead with the heel of his hand. 'Of course, he'll have seen that. If we haul it down it looks as though you've made contact. Let it go. We have another one. Slip the pawl in daylight and let it float away. That tells nothing. It looks like an accident.'

Miranda said, 'Why not leave it tethered here. That way it looks as though the cone's still here. Like the last watch of Hero.'

Alvirez ceremonially kissed her on both cheeks. Then he asked, 'How far along to the cradles?'

'It's a big bay. Perhaps ten miles. Not far if we could sail across. There's no way of knowing whether the actual sea coast follows the line of the cliff. But it's more than likely.'

'Start at first light then. Give you time to take in another bucketful of the Dolon soup.'

'We'll do that.'

Fletcher stretched himself cautiously, feeling as though he might split his skin. He went along to one of the tank compartments where Karen was lying on an acceleration couch in the narrow floor space.

She was sleeping peacefully. Her hair was spread on the low swell of the head rest, in a bell-shaped auburn curve, which his mathematician's mind told him was normal distribution with the mean centred at the arch of her left eyebrow. It was the sort of perfection that was typical of her personality. He moved a thick silky swathe of it as a gesture in the direction of 'sampling error'. She briefly opened her eyes and was awake enough to say 'I love you.' Then she drifted back into sleep and he backed painfully out of the confined space into the corridor.

Susan too was asleep. She had taken a beating on the haul through the swamps and was the least recovered. Her face was still very pale and she had not yet fully relaxed.

Chad was probably most affected by the heat. He never knew how long he had gone on with no refrigeration at all from his suit. Otherwise he was well on the way back to normal.

Dag made a reservation that he alone would go out with Alvirez and Craig, if there was not a great improvement in Chad's skin condition over the next fourteen hours. Certainly the chafing, inevitable under space gear, would be extremely uncomfortable in its present state. But he knew his man and made no suggestion of it.

Chad said, 'What I want to do, mainly, is to get hold of Ven Smith and twist his stupid head off. I should have done it after Alec's death. I reckon I was pretty sure then. It would have saved a lot of trouble.'

'He wasn't entirely to blame for that. But on this last effort, there was no immediate compulsion from the force bands. Not as far as I know. It means that Records need to put a more stringent ruling out on Suggestibility levels. Any crew I take out after this will rate "A" on that item.'

'That might be expensive. It could rule out some good men.'

'Nothing could be more expensive than total loss and we've come near that. If we get away now we'll leave Alec and Dan Munro, Randle, Bennett and Pete Anders. That's a pretty good butcher's bill for a few points on a personality rating. And it isn't finished yet. There's Len there. And I very much doubt whether Myers and Smith will get back.'

'You've got a point. Try selling it to some chairborne wonder like Spencer though. Space personnel are very rare and expensive birds. The only clear case to an admin type would be if a man was physically too big to get through a hatch.'

'You should know about that.'

'Not any more. That reminds me. Do you think our Valkyrie could bring up another bowl of whatever it is?'

Nobody was very far from anybody else in the small cone section. A great deal of the narrowing point was filled solid with electronic equipment and the long tanks took up most of the remaining space. Miranda was along with a shallow dish of steaming thick liquid before Dag had time to pass on the request.

The couches were not gymbol mounted. Normally only one crewman had a take-off station in the cone. Other beds had been put in to accommodate personnel on the long trek. Chad sat up slowly and began to drink his new ration with flattering evidence of enjoyment. When the cone rolled a good two feet along its sandy anchorage, a generous half pint of hot poultice slapped down on the reddened skin of his bare chest.

His reactions were a living proof that he was fully recovered. Some basic English assertions brought a startled look even to Miranda's face and then he went on in Gaelic though the tone was still unmistakable. He rampaged through the capsule in a frenzy. In the confined space it was like being shut up with a mad bull. Illogically, he was blaming Smith for it and his ultimate spate of self-expression included another promise to twist his basic head off.

By the time there was relative calm, Alvirez was in a suit and ready to investigate. Dag said, 'Take it easy, John.

It's probably a land crab. We haven't seen any dinosaurs down below the cliff top. One thing's for sure, you can shoot where you like, there's no chance of hitting anything that matters.'

Ten minutes later, Alvirez was back inside. 'There's nothing near the cone. There could be anything at all three feet away from it in any direction; but there's nothing nearer than that. It must have been imagination.'

Only the fact that Miranda was virtually kneeling on him in the course of first-aid ministrations kept Chad from homicide.

The blanket outside had notched itself up several tones to a medium grey, when the four men set out. Fletcher had brought his log up to date by written notes which he could later dictate into the sealed recorder. He left the tablet with the incompleted entry, 'Day 71 . . . remaining crew members in two parties. Karen Evander, Susan Yardley and Miranda Dolon remaining in the stranded Cone Section. Fletcher, Alvirez, Fergusson and Craig leaving to contact the ship, estimated to lie south along the shore of the bay. Distant about fifteen miles. . . .'

Karen had made great strides towards recovery. There was something on her mind, however, which she tried to bring into consciousness and could not. Just before he left, she said, 'There's something on the tip of my tongue. I feel that I owe you an apology, an explanation about something.'

'Don't worry about it. Anything you do is all right as far as I'm concerned.'

'Not this thing. It's something terrible, but I don't know what.'

'I think I know what it is and believe me it doesn't matter at all.'

'Honestly?'

'I'll tell you what it was sometime. Just now there's a lot to do. You're senior here. Keep this log. If we don't get back you should make an effort to go north. Miranda can make some kind of homing signal, given time. Then you would have to wait until you were picked up. But it won't come to that.'

'If you didn't come back, I shouldn't care either way.'

'We both know that an attempt to get back has to be made down to the last one.'

They were close together in the narrow confines of a tank bay. He felt the build-up of sensitivity which was a prelude to thought transfer between them. That would give her access to the knowledge that she had tried to kill him. He kissed her briefly on the lips. Firm, hard, quick, with only seconds to register their familiar texture and the seal it gave to their confidence in each other. Then he joined the other three in the hot mist.

At first they followed the water's edge, splashing along in a few inches of water, feet sinking invisibly in the soft sand. They were roped on short lines less than six feet apart, but each in the isolation of the mist. When Dag was brought to a halt by a sheer face of rock looming in front of him, the others piled up at his back. Alvirez appeared out of the mist like a truncated wraith when his visor was eighteen inches away.

Dag said, 'We'll move down into the water. Going over this would bring us into view. It's an outside chance, but we shouldn't take it.'

The rock was still rising sheer on his left when the beach dropped away into an unknown depth of water and left them afloat like corks on a seine net. Dag took up a slow clumsy crawl, keeping well in to test progress against the rock. It was over a hundred yards and seemed several miles before the blank wall gave way to a low spur which could be climbed.

Alvirez said, 'We'll have to watch that on the way back. Could wreck us.'

The other side of the spur was less cut back and, within

fifteen yards, the water shoaled and they were following the line of the sandy beach again. That was the pattern for the next two hours. Long stretches of slogging footwork then a detour round an obstruction which stuck a rocky finger out to sea.

They halted for a ten minute spell in a close circle for the comfort of visual proof that there were other people in this silent sub-world. There was no heat problem with the suits working to specification; but there was the psychological one of dependence on such a frail link. Each one knew that he was carried over conditions intolerable for human life on a flimsy raft. And the claustrophobic mist was no encouragement. Two short force bands, carrying the disintegrating rhythm, had been crossed. When they were through the last one, Alvirez said, 'I've got a hunch about these things. I believe the causative agent is nearer than we think. After all, the next land mass is hundreds of miles away and the energy required to transmit that distance would be colossal. It's something within a hundred miles and powerful at that.'

'Could be.' Chad was impressed by the power argument. 'But it's not going to matter if we stay outside the bands.'

They went on. It was neither day nor night. Trudging legs half-hidden, a womb world, a negating destroying world; the rope links were a thin thread of reassuring sanity. At the end of the second stint, they could have been still outside the cone or a thousand miles from it. Nothing had changed. They were hamsters in an exercise wheel. Dag said, 'We've done ten miles or more. This next leg ought to find it. Then it's transport back.'

Loneliness built up to its peak of introspection. Even the most gruelling of early training tests had been nothing at all compared with what they were experiencing. Dag began a long conversation with Alvirez on training method. They agreed that no simulator could come near the real conditions, because no trial of personnel could be a trial to destruction which was what they faced. Every training situation ended with tea and crumpet and nothing could prevent the trainee knowing that it would be so.

Alvirez was going on to outline a blood freezing set up, which he believed would do the trick, when Fletcher said, 'If you ever get that on a programme you'll be the Black Mullah of the service. But you can give it a rest. We're home and dry.'

The ragged side of *Santa Maria* was blocking the way ahead.

If they could have seen what they were doing, it would have been fairly straightforward; but moving the clumsy hulk back into the water, without the help of the power which had been used to beach it, and in the perpetual blind-fold of the mist, was a fantastic operation. The long shallow cradle, seen only in small sections as they moved slowly around it, seemed immense. Chad unhooked himself from the bead chain and concentrated on the power unit. When he was satisfied that it was operational, he sent out a short hetero-dyne howl on his intercom. Dag had ruled speech out, think-ing that they were now near enough to the ship to make it easily identifiable on the control console.

The other three had used levers and rollers to move the heavy shell backwards. When it floated free they climbed aboard and joined Chad in the stern.

Speaking on the person-to-person link, he arranged with Dag to move off dead slow ahead. Alvirez was sent forward with a lead line to call the depths. He was to signal by two clicks for starboard helm, one click for port.

Craig, who spent most of the time in a dour silence made a rare break to ask, 'How do we find this place again?'

'We don't need the exact spot. Anywhere below the plat-eau, with a fairly wide tolerance, will do. Once we have the ship, it's a matter of getting the cone upstairs.'

The first of many snags ended the conversation. Even at dead slow, the time lag on the course signals was too great and *Santa Maria* had ploughed into the beach again before Chad could correct it. But they were making better time than on the trek out. Levers and odd timbers from the wrecked *Pinta* lay in the well. They would be needed to make derricks to lift the cone on to its floating platform. Without their usual power sources it would be difficult enough. Just now they came in useful to shove off from shore. Craig and Fletcher stood on either side of Mark Twain ready to fend off.

After the fourth grounding, Dag took a chance on the course and cut across the bay to hit one of the long moles which ran out to sea. They they moved along its flank, fending off and probing for the turn. Thereafter, the pattern was set, until the last stretch, when it was a slow grind along the beach with Craig walking on a lead like a canal boat horse. He found their objective, as they had found everything else, by walking into it.

They had put in a twelve hour day without food. Fletcher and Fergusson were rapidly falling back into complete exhaustion. Inside, they found that Susan had been bending her gourmet's brain to the vegetable problem. She had devised a kind of solid cutlet fried in vegetable oil. In the light, in the freedom from the heavy gear, surrounded by the solid evidence of normality, it was easier to opt for life; but the silence of the four men communicated itself even to Miranda and the weight of the endless difficulties of the environment seemed to enclose them like a straight jacket.

Working with a kind of blind ferocity to get themselves out of the tomb life of the mist, they took only two days to devise and operate lifting gear and move the cone on to the cradle. There was nothing to keep them. Night and day were abstractions. They poled along in shallow water to the first long spur. By midnight, they had reached a point which Dag estimated was within a mile of the original landfall of the

Santa Maria. Under radio silence, they took lines ashore and made fast.

Reveille was late on day 74. After breakfast, Fletcher and Alvirez prepared to take a look over the mist. Without the power-suit to do its levitation act, there was going to be some hard graft.

Miranda said, 'You need three. Let me come, John.' Alvirez looked at Dag for confirmation and got a nod.

'All right. But get a wriggle on.'

It was unnecessary advice on several counts. In the event she was ready first. They laid a thin guide line over the beach to lead them back and hit the cliff where it went straight up like a mortarless wall. Dag said, 'We can take a look and see where the top is. But it's a fairly even ledge about twenty-five feet up.'

He put his back to the wall and Alvirez climbed to stand on his shoulders. Then Miranda climbed the column. As her visor levelled with theirs, the unmistakable message in her expressive eyes was, 'Indispensible.'

She stayed so long looking into Alvirez's goldfish bowl that Dag, who was on a direct speech link to him, said, 'For god's sake, John, get that girl moving. Like the man said, there's a time for everything.'

The message that filtered down was precise enough. She could see the balloon hovering over their old camp site. The ledge was well out of reach. Fifty yards right there was an irregularity in the cliff face which looked promising.

She dropped down again with only a token stop to see how Alvirez was getting on and they moved over to the fault. This time it was possible to climb. Miranda had superb balance even in the clumsy suit and went up first like a cat. Then they were standing on the ledge and Alvirez was taking his first look for some time over a reasonable stretch of Pelorus. They marked the spot which would take them down to the invisible guide-line below and then moved off farther right.

Less than fifty yards away, round a slight bluff, the lines and tackles which had been used before were still hanging down the cliff face.

So far, it was unlikely that they would have been seen. But the next stage was crucial. On it would depend whether or not any future move could have a surprise value. In the end, Dag faced the fact that there was no way round it. It was one of those chances which had to be taken.

The view from the rim of rock was unchanged. Two thirds complete. *Interstellar Two-Five* reared its slender needle from the hummock mounds of dinosaur. Nothing moved. After the long session in the featureless mist, the jungle wall seemed more pulsating with colour than before. But it was the stationary colour of a tourist poster.

The top platform was empty. *Two-Five* had no armament which could be directed from inside. He decided to carry the reconnaissance to the door. Alvirez came up and lay beside him, then Miranda, impatient to see the ship.

Dag said, 'It's long range for a small Laser, but give me cover. If anyone tries to use that flame-thrower on top, drop him.'

He covered the hundred yards to a crumbling flank of dinosaur at a stumbling run. Then he waited as a blinding shower of hot rain seethed down. When the rock had steamed dry, he worked round into the open and found that the sheltering tripod was within reach of another straight run.

There was still no sign of life from the ship. No movement at any port. He began to move. Ten yards from home, he ran into a force band with the impact of a physical blow. The pulsating, destructive rhythm sent a jagged searing flare of crimson through his brain and he fell in an unco-ordinated sprawl.

CHAPTER TEN

JOHN ALVIREZ was in an impossible position. He saw
Fletcher make the cover of the tattered grey mound, then the
rain came down and he waited impatiently to get a clear
view. When the ship was visible again through the rapidly
thinning steam, he saw that the silver suit had gone forward.
He knew that he could not possibly hit any target at that
extreme range and could only give covering fire if he moved
up. He decided to ignore orders and move in. With Miranda
beside him, he had reached the same dumb shelter before the
last of the mist cleared away. He crawled from its lee to
take a look at the ship and saw Dag, lying face down, thirty
yards out.

Miranda said, 'I'm sure it's nothing from the ship. It must
be a force band with something special in it. I'll get him.'
Before he could stop her, she was running towards the prone
figure. When she was almost there, she stopped and moved
gingerly, an inch at a time. She was an arm's length from the
feet, when she jerked back as if there was an invisible hedge
of bare electrodes.

There was no sign or movement from the ship. He ran out
to join her.

'It's a force field all right. The strongest we've met yet. I
don't think we can get to him without blacking out.'

Alvirez was already making a casting loop. He threw it
out to catch on to projections in the gear carried by the back
harness. At the second throw, he got a bite and they pulled
the limp body back over the threshold.

He said, 'He's well out. Needs to be back inside and that quickly. Help me to get him across my back, then go ahead and bring Chad and Craig out.'

Dag Fletcher came back to consciousness with the scene before the ship alive on his retina and struggled to continue his forward run to the shelter of the tripod legs. Then the image melted unaccountably into the oval of Karen's face and she was saying, 'Easy, Dag. Take it easy.'

'It's all right.' He sat up slowly.

'The others?'

'They brought you out. John thinks the ship's deserted. There wasn't a move from it and you were all sitting ducks for long enough.'

'That figures. The bands move slowly. One finally got to the ship. It would hit Smith and Myers before they could get out. This one's a killer. We can't even move through it.' He raised his voice. 'John.'

'Here, present.' Alvirez appeared at the opening of the bay.

'We can't afford to blunder into that band. Get Chad working on a probe. Like a mine detector. An inclinometer tripping a relay and lighting a bulb. On a six foot rod. Then we can feel our way round.'

Chad Fergusson appeared behind Alvirez and packed in beside him in the narrow opening.

'I heard that. It's a variant on the old song about a hole in a bucket. We need an inclinometer to guide us to the work shop where the materials to make an inclinometer are all stacked up.'

'You don't have to be too particular. Surely there's a needle in a dial on some of this gear. Magnetise it and put in a contact. We need it, as of now, to protect us here. If that band moves this way, we want enough warning to get out. As soon as it's ready we'll take another look at the ship.'

Chad made two and left one outside the cone to trip a signal in the event of any change of magnetic field in the neighbourhood. The four men went up on to the plateau with a Heath Robinson contraption on a pole. A bulb glowed and a buzzer sounded in the head-sets when it was thrust into changing lines of force.

It was clear that there was nothing to fear from the ship. They made their way through the morgue and Chad had gratifying success from his probe. He moved left and found a clear way. Then they went on. In half an hour, they had plotted the extent of the force band. It dropped like a broad shaft of sunlight at a forty-five degree angle and left a pool of power in an ellipse round the ship.

Two-Five effectively sealed off: as if a cordon of troops had been drawn round it.

Dag said, 'We'll bring the cone up to the ledge. That way we're out of the mist and one move nearer its final home. Then we can think about these force bands. I'm sick to death of being on the receiving end.'

Craig had been chewing over the data in his dour silent way. He came out with, 'The angle here is near enough 45°. If it's a regular curve, we know where the other end will be. It might be worth taking a look.'

Alvirez said, 'This is where we need transport. That's a good idea, though.'

Working without any powered winch, it took the best part of a day to drag the cone to the foot of the cliff and then lift it on to the ledge.

Refrigeration loss by using the simple hatch openings was beginning to put a heavy strain on the capsule's plant. It was in any case only an ancilliary unit, designed to operate on an emergency basis when the main system in the power pack was disconnected. Time was beginning to run out.

On the morning of day 76, Dag checked the limits of the force field and found them unmoved. He said, 'The line of the arc follows the cliff, we'll have to take a look. I believe this is a static agent, or there would have been direct intervention. Perhaps we can change its mind.'

Karen asked, 'How far away is the other end?'

'It depends on the height of the curve, but possibly within ten miles.'

'Anything over a day's march is going to be pretty dicey. Two and a half days out is getting close to maximum.'

Chad said, 'This is mule country. We need a pack animal. What about that balloon. It could carry spare gear. Flame-thrower even.'

Miranda put in, 'I don't fancy being left in this place. Make it a full party.'

It was clear that this view was general. In any event, further losses of personnel would put any move with *Two-Five* out of court. They might as well stick together.

Timed at 0930 hours, the last entry in the temporary log, left in the cone for a problematic posterity, listed the seven survivors and said that they were setting out in an attempt to trace the source of the energy emissions carried by the magnetic field of Pelorus which was denying access to the ship.

The balloon was balanced to keep a load of spares and food about ten feet off the ground and was towed along in turn by the last two in the column. Craig and Miranda took first stint and the small party made six miles in two and a half hours, before Dag signalled a halt.

The nature of the ground was unchanged. On the left the wall of jungle was an unbroken blaze of colour. On the right, the cliff edge and the indefinite horizon, where the cinnamon sky melted into the fleece below. Behind them, the ship, with its ring of mounds, sinking now as the frequent rain squalls washed away the putrescent flesh. It looked curiously stunted without the cone. But nothing could detract from the mathematical perfection of its lines. Ahead, there seemed to be nothing new. It was a fool's errand.

The next lap brought no change in the overall view. A section of petrified sastrugi added some difficulty underfoot and slowed them down. They were all silent. Whatever was opposing them was too nebulous to create a positive reaction. It was impossible to hate a void.

Then Chad's device began to earn its keep. They had to weave backwards and forwards, between the cliff edge and the jungle wall, picking a way through an increasing concentration of force bands. The strip of rocky plateau was widening. Sometimes only a narrow gulley separated force bands. The clicking of the detector was a constant background accompaniment as Dag led through the invisible maze.

Journey's end arrived unexpectedly and for some minutes was not recognised.

A dark line ahead stretching across the whole width of the mile-wide plateau, separated itself out as a vast depression in the rock. When they reached the edge, they were hemmed in by force bands at arm's length on either side. Below them was an immense circular fault like a sunken amphitheatre.

Karen said uncertainly, 'It can't be.' She handed her recording lenses to Dag and he looked more closely at the grey tumulus which filled the floor below them. It was almost a mile long and half a mile wide, rising to a central height of a hundred feet or more and curving away in a bland, grey symmetry like an inflated pale skin. When he brought up the glasses, he saw that there was no continuity about it. It was composed of countless myriads of discrete and individual termites, pale grey, elongated ovals about three inches long. The whole mass was seething and pullulating with rhythmic life.

Miranda said, 'Look at that. By the jungle edge.'

It was clear enough to see the action with the naked eye, but through the glasses it was plain that the dinosaur was very old and feeble. It had come out from the multi-coloured backdrop and was standing on the edge of the pit. It weaved its immense head from side to side, as though in doubt, then it shuffled forward. Straight ahead, until it pitched down in a sheer drop. There was one check as it struck the projection of a ledge, twenty feet up, then it fell to the ground almost on the perimeter of the grey mass.

Through the glasses Dag could see that it had fallen into a boneyard. What depth of bone there was, it would be impossible to say. But it had joined a thick deposit of previous leapers. Even before the next move, he had an inkling of what it would be.

The grey mass appeared to expand elastically in the direction of the new boy. It flowed sluggishly round and over until the dead monster was engulfed and invisible. Then it slowly and glutinously retracted itself. The white bones sank in an indisinguishable heap to join the rest on the charnel house floor. The whole process had taken under five minutes.

Dag said, 'This mass is acting like a brain. It *is* a brain. A human brain has ten thousand million individual cells. This one has the capacity of thousands of human brains added together. You can see how it might have started up. This is a burial ground for old dinosaurs. It would be a food store for primitive forms of life. Then it's the centre of these special force bands, which can create a bond for mental co-operation between separate brains. It would grow. First a few would act together and then more, until it produced this overwhelming organisation. The communal brain has produced an emergent mind, which can now guarantee its own survival. It can perpetuate itself. It's virtually immortal. Millions of its components can die and be replaced. It regulates its physical host.'

Karen said, 'It's moving this way.'

The grey mass was thickening at the edge nearest to them. Then it spread out again into its original form and it had certainly moved nearer to them. Then it repeated the manœuvre to the left.

Alvirez said, 'That looks like a compensating movement.

It's got a built-in system for tracking the main force band. Of course, it has to stay centred on that to keep alive.'

'The force field is its eyes and ears.' Miranda was leaning forward, fascinated by the communications possibilities of the network. 'It could track anyone anywhere on Pelorus as they crossed the bands.'

Clicking in the headsets brought Dag, belatedly, to the danger. Of course it could track them. And now it would know precisely where they were.

Chad said, 'That's from behind. We're closed in. There's only one way and that's forward.'

'We can give it something else to think about. Pull the balloon in and unpack the flame-thrower. But quickly.'

Retreating a foot at a time, they had a narrow, shrinking platform, less than nine feet square, when Dag sent the first searing stream to cut a narrow swathe through the grey barrow. He loaded and fired until the tube was too hot to handle. The mass below had been cauterised into numberless small hillocks. Myriads of its constituent units had been destroyed, much of it would be outside the force field. In the centre of the heap, as a kind of nucleus, was a fragmentary skeletal structure.

'That was a space ship.' Karen's positive identification revealed the pattern. It could be so.

'That would kill off a few. Retro rockets blasting down would just about clear the area.'

'When the brain re-established itself, it would definitely have a thing about space-ships. Treat them as hostile.'

'This will confirm its worst suspicions.'

The creeping barrage of force lines which had halted during the firing, began to move again.

Dag said, 'There's still enough mass down there to operate like several human brains. But maybe we've checked it enough to decrease its long-range strength.'

The rear wall was still coming in. They were standing in

a compact group. No more movement was possible except over the edge.

The familiar gauze curtain effect drew rapidly over them. Craig suddenly began to walk forward. The devastating rhythm was no longer there. Only a compulsive force towards the pit.

The rest felt it and set their minds against it. They resisted it, but they could not positively begin to walk away. It was a balance of forces. Stalemate. Alvirez and Fergusson were holding Craig as he tried to struggle over the edge.

Karen began to unseal her visor. Dag was standing next to her and saw the action. She said, 'The combined mind will be strong enough.'

There would not be long. When the two visors opened, a fierce gust of furnace heat drove at their faces. But over the physical pain, they felt the surge of power build up between them as their foreheads touched. The emergent mind grew from their deep unity willing co-operation and in some way beyond an individual comprehension was fighting back along the channel of the force band to the very centre of the pit's intelligence. Craig stopped struggling. Minutes passed. How long could they maintain the third force, which grew from their two brains. Karen suddenly fell away from him and Miranda was beside her, resealing the hot metal of the visor. Fletcher was still able to close his own with fumbling fingers. Then they were going back. Clicks from the inclinometer traced the frequent crossings of force bands. They carried no overtone of menace.

Dag said through swollen lips. 'The quicker we move the better. That heap will regroup itself. Nothing more sure. We don't know how long we've got. This goes on report. An I.G.O. patrol can come in and clear up.'

Interstellar Two-Five stood like a silver pointer in the clearing mists of a rain squall. A remnant remained wreathing in tendrils from the heating rocket tubes. Another mound had joined the shrinking hillocks of reptile leather, remnants of cradles, fittings, equipment, everything that could be spared. The ship had been stripped down to essentials.

Four days of intensive effort had gone into the final stage. Dag had driven everyone flat out.

'We have the initiative now. But maggot brain will try again. It won't leave a potential danger loose on its territory without a struggle. Time is not on our side.'

The force field round the ship had been negative, carrying no overtone of threat. They lifted the cone and put it in place so that they could break through from an inside hatch. It was a lengthy job. Susan and Miranda had done most of it, to let the rest get on with the assembly work. Finally they were through and Dag dropped in with a Laser ready. It was unnecessary.

Smith and Myers were dead in the control room. Smith's face was set in a rigid pattern of utter agony. Myers had taken an oblivion pill. He was sitting at the communications sub-console with his hands out in front of him, and the empty torpedo-shaped phial was on the table top. Whom the Gods would destroy, they first make mad.

Len Robertshaw was in his cabin. The door was still locked. He had not been able to get out. Lying in a heap against the door it looked as though he had been hammering on it, before the destructive rhythm blacked him out.

The three were put in disposal bags and given a narrow tomb in the hard rock. It was the last outside chore before Dag called the crew together for a pre-blast-off briefing.

Miranda had been processing data and checking through Len's calculations with a new weight table. She gave 2005 hours as an optimum take-off time.

They took up positions round the chart spread. Each console would have its operator. PILOT, CO-PILOT, Susan in the NAVIGATION seat, Chad at POWER, Miranda at COM-

MUNICATIONS. Karen had her SPECIALIST desk. Craig was in for the conference, but would have to take over the secondary panel in the power pack, when they were ready to go. It was a viable crew. Just.

Dag put in a preamble beginning, 'Day 81,' and then went on, 'It is established that the optimum time for take-off will be 2005 hours. There is fuel to mount an escape velocity. The aim is to put the ship in an orbit round Talos. From there we will refuel by tender and land as originally intended. Stores as follows are jettisoned to save weight.'

He went on to enumerate the items piled below. Then he stopped and looked round the group. With some sense of occasion, the three girls had put on ceremonial tabards for the meeting. Miranda's blonde hair was in startling contrast to black silk, shot with bronze, Susan in vermilion was a mediaeval page, Karen was a Maillol nymph in translucent lime green. There was one hour before blast-off.

He went on, 'At this stage, does any member of the crew wish to go on record with any opinion that would be contrary to that course of action?'

There was no indecision on any face. Tired and jaded, they were nevertheless utterly determined. He released the record button and said, 'When we reassemble here it will be for take-off. There will be no time for speeches. Whichever way it goes, I am glad to have had command of this ship. No one ever worked with better people. It's a simple issue now. Either we break through or we don't. There won't be anything left to make a controlled landing back on Pelorus. As soon as we get over the communication barrier, Miranda can intensify watch and transmission on 1420. Once in orbit round Talos, it shouldn't take long. Back here at 1920 for section checks.'

Alvirez said, in a mock-official tone to debunk his own sincerity, 'I thank you from the bottom of my heart and from Miranda's also. You've done a great job.' The meeting broke up and they moved out.

Karen remained at the chart spread and Dag joined her. They looked at the scanner pictures. Miranda had sent up the tallest probe from the tip of the cone and they had a panoramic view of a hundred square miles. Even the lip of the mind pit was visible as a darker line on the plateau. A movement there, on the fringe of the vegetation, suggested that its food supplies were still coming up.

'We're not leaving before time.'

She turned and faced him. Without haste they moved together. Each was kinaesthetically aware of the total form of the other's body. Without speech she communicated, 'Whichever way it goes, I'm glad we've had this.'

'It isn't over yet.'

With everyone in full gear, and the acceleration couches down, the control cabin of *Interstellar Two-Five* looked professionally stacked. The main chronometer was coming up to 2000 hours, when Dag began the round of routine clearances from the command console.

Miranda switched in the retractor gear and the long antenna slid back into its sheath. Then she cleared the computers and came up in a clear pseudo-naïve soprano, 'Communications. All Systems Go.'

Chad Fergusson made a final check along the serried ranks of dials on the power console and spoke briefly on his extension to Craig. Then he said shortly, 'Power. All Systems Go.'

Susan Yardley double checked every tell-tale on the navigator's panel. For her it was the first time as a key link in a take off. But her voice was steady and confident with, 'Navigation. All Systems Go.'

Dag transferred the cleared systems and pulled in the robot mechanism for count down. Alarm bleeps started up in empty cabins. Miranda had reduced the scanner picture to a maximum scale view of the immediate area of the ship. Great petals of steam were curving from the tripod legs to screen the ship in a white calix. The bleeps gave place to clicks and the sweep hand came into the red quadrant. The clicks ceased. The hiss became a gathering roar, the white flower glowed incandescent orange and the ship began its slow, graceful lift. Casually, then with gathering momentum it flung itself into the darkening sky of Pelorus. In the scanner the pad was marked by the tall blazing chimney of the log gantry.

There was no conversation. Everyone knew that the next crisis was only minutes distant. The immediate danger of blast-off had been passed. The huge motor was still developing maximum thrust. It was a question of how long it would go on doing just that.

Flatness gave way to curvature below them and the island of Tragasus was a blue-green map feature with its rock shelf rising from a bed of mist. Then the mist's northern limits appeared and the wine-dark Polyphontine Sea. To the south the mist went on in a continuous blanket to the equatorial continental mass, edged by the improbable white ridges of the Leucophanes.

Karen was methodically taking stills for the Pilotage Manual archives. It kept a third of her mind off the main issue. But the other two-thirds was overwhelmed by the great question mark.

Chad was watching his dials. Fuel was dropping into the red sector. He could not maintain the thrust for many seconds more. Then it had gone, according to the gauges, and they were going on some bonus which had been built in to the mechanism. Automatically, crash warning bleeps began to sound through the empty cabins of the ship.

Fletcher and Alvirez, powerless at the command console, were willing the ship to carry on. They were so nearly through. Miraculously the thrust had not died. Chad had given up. Blind chance had taken over the propulsion unit.

Everyone, keyed to the vibrant note of the ship, was waiting for the change of pitch when the thrust would begin to die. Miranda was still feeding the computers. She was filling the Senior Communications role without hesitation. What she lacked in Robertshaw's experience, she made up with a kind of mathematical intuition. She was utterly single-minded and when the tapes told her they had won out, her report was immediate and on the PILOT channel. Only when she had done that did she switch to CO-PILOT and say, 'Which precise part of South America had you in mind, John?'

Then the rockets died and *Interstellar Two-Five* ghosted on in a trajectory which was bringing Talos from a winking red dot into a brilliant florin of white light.

It would be three days before the ellipse of their orbit took them near enough to be within range for a stubby fuelling capsule to come out from Talos. Details were already known to Talos control. Miranda had transmitted a complete, computer digested, flight plot. The ground organisation would be lining it up, so that the squat projectile would track round with *Two-Five* at the exact distance and speed to make docking it a practicable matter. Without power to manoeuvre the ship it was going to be one of the trickiest things in astral navigation. Even with Robertshaw at the computers it would have been a dicey thing. Miranda was unruffled.

Dag Fletcher was checking out personnel files, filling in time on the routine chore of duty officer in the control cabin, writing FINIS on too many good men to make any landfall comfortable. Under DOLON, Miranda, he put a brief note. There would be more later, when he finalised his voyage report; but, for now, he recorded the highlights of her contribution to the enterprise. If she stayed in the SPACE WING, she was a certainty for a top communications post. He would take her as Senior Communications on any mission, in spite of age and the AMOR tag. Though it looked as though she was going to settle for John Alvirez.

Craig was a problem. He had only just missed being in the Smith/Myers group. Experience had to be the teacher. That, or there would be no safety. He pressed the recorder button and put a postscript on Craig's tape.

'Technically well qualified. Every proof of first-class ability as an engineer and suitable for promotion on ground establishments. Note, however, suggestibility rating. Not a reliable crewman for extended deep space flight.'

That would finish Craig for space crew. It was unfortunate, but he could not put some future ship in peril for any sentimental reason.

When he came to EVANDER, Karen, he had to try to erase her image from his mind. Try to. It was not finally possible and an Esquiline Venus was a shadowy background figure to his deliberations. Everything was good from the professional angle. Her contribution to the trek had been first-class in every way. She was the completely dependable lieutenant. But she had tried to kill him. What about that? Put down baldly in the record, it would cancel every other entry. Put down *anyway*, it would take some explanation to minimise its severity.

Why record it at all? But he was doing a job now, which he would expect other captains to do, according to the rules. Rules of honour. Which was pretty archaic when you came down to it. But there was no twisted way round it. You could call it honour or integrity or duty or even professionalism; but there was a compulsion from some deep central core of personality, that would not be humbugged or side tracked. It would have to go in. After all Susan and Chad had been on the same line and they had not tried to drill a hole in him. But then they were not in love with him. That was it, of course. All part of the love/hate syndrome. It was his own fault for having an emotional relationship with a crew member. So any entry there would have to couple with it his share of responsibility. Also she had saved his life. How many times did you have to save a life to cancel out an attempt to take it?

There was a slight movement at the hatch. Without giving any indication that he had heard, he slipped the microtapes into their tube and dropped it in its slot in the desk, then he turned in a continuation of the movement to meet Karen as she came through.

She stopped dead, with recognition of a coincidence of place and movement. There was one thing missing in the repeat performance. This time no Laser came up to challenge her. But the relays clicked along the mental circuits and she said, 'Friend, I think.' At the same moment she knew what it was that was bothering her as a half-remembered thing. For a brief second, she was back in an intolerable shroud of weariness and pain and falling down a sliding curtain of steaming water, with only one consuming thought in mind. She said, 'I didn't want to kill *you*. I wanted to kill whatever it was that was making you go on.'

'I know that.'

A new thought struck her. 'This puts you in a spot. It has to go on report.'

'Yes.'

She made it easy. 'Of course, it has. Don't give it a thought. I have no executive ambitions. So long as it doesn't alter anything between us.'

'How could it do that? It's an oblique compliment. "Every man kills the thing he loves." But you don't mind me stopping you in extreme cases?'

'No.'

Her tone was so self doubting that he left the desk and met her in the small open space in the centre of the consoles. She would not meet his eyes, until he was holding her and lifting her chin. In spite of her equality in professionalism, he realised that this was one time when only a practical and primitive demonstration would carry conviction.

The continents and oceans of Talos were spread out like a

large size relief globe. Precise to its split second timing, the fuel canister lobbed up, to end the stellar loneliness of *Two-Five* and Fergusson went out with Craig to bring it in. Later, Miranda worked out a trajectory for it and it was fired, by remote control, to drop into an ocean on a map reference, which she sent in to Talos control. Then they had a manoeuvrable ship again.

Talos offered a flight programme to bring them in. Dag sent a signal that they were fully operational and could work it out. Acting Chief Communications rewarded him with a look of such pure gratitude, that it was worth hazarding the ship. When *Two-Five* blazed its way down with perfect positioning, on its designated pad, Miranda had qualified under the most stringent test she was ever likely to meet.

There was a moment, before Quarantine came aboard the cooling ship. They were out of space gear and waiting for their microcosm to be invaded and absorbed. In the silent cabin, they were occupied with their own thoughts. Each one knew that this was simultaneously shared. However long they lived, whatever else they did, there would always be a kinship between them as strong as a blood tie. Then the officials were in and the Earth consul was inviting them to use the Consulate as their base. Life had moved on as it always does, on one level or another, to the next thing, whatever has gone before.